Survivor Guilt

SURVIVOR GUILT

HAIG TAHTA

BLACK
APOLLO
PRESS

First published in Great Britain by
Black Apollo Press, 2011

ISBN: 9781900355735

A CIP catalogue record of this book is available at
the British Library.

For information regarding our other titles, please
go to our website:
www.blackapollo.com

Contents

Chapter 1

The death of Raffi

It was Vahan who was the first on the scene, finding the body of his younger brother early in the morning when he padded across to the small modernised bathroom which they shared. The family house was a three-storey building on Osmanli Sokag just a few hundred yards down from Taksim Square. The blood from the young man's wrists had flowed into the bath, though a small quantity had run onto the floor and was congealing round his body. It was clear that even in death Raffi was obsessed with the family trait of careful tidiness. Kneeling on the floor at the edge of the bath, he appeared to have slashed both his wrists draping his arms over the edge of the bathtub. As the blood had seeped away his body had eventually weakened, and as he died he had fallen back onto the floor, where the last spurts of blood before his heart finally stopped had flowed and dried on the floor.

Vahan stood at the door in a state of complete shock. His initial reaction was not the overwhelming distress at the death of his brother so much as the sight of all the blood and self-inflicted violence in the midst of domesticity that left him speechless and frozen to the spot. This was 1924 in Constantinople. With the establishment of the new Republic, under the leadership of

General Mustapha Kemal, a semblance of peace and order had finally arrived as the old Ottoman Empire began to fade into memory. The killings and bloodshed of the last 12 years as the Empire crumbled to its death was fast becoming history. So the violence of the scene in the bathroom, in contrast to the peace and order settling over public life, made the shock that much greater.

The blood on the floor had long since congealed – Raffi's heart must have stopped sometime in the middle of the night. Vahan felt the nausea rising in his stomach and then at last he began to scream as an uncontrollable trembling seized his body. His father, Garabed, came running up the stairs wrapped in a white bathrobe. He had been dealing with his own morning ablutions in the large old-fashioned stone hamal on the first floor below. Vahan's strangulated cries, while not all that loud had the timbre of terror about it which caused Garabed to drop everything and rush up the stairs.

Vahan's step-brother Ara, younger than Raffi, came running down the stairs from the top floor. He took one look into the bathroom where Garabed was now leaning over the body of his son, and then held Vahan tightly to control his shivering. The servants appeared. Ara let out a sharp cry and released Vahan as he saw their little sister, Satenig, appear at the top of the stairs, wide-eyed at all the commotion. She began to walk down. With a bound Ara ran up to her, making sure that she did not witness the horror in the little bathroom. He murmured soothing words, "It's all right – it's all right. Your brother has had an accident. No, no, I don't think he would like you to see. Just stay with me – Daddy will look after it." He held on to her tightly and led her back to her room.

Whatever the drama, whatever the pain of circumstances, life goes on. Between them Garabed and Ara called the Doctor, sorted out the local police, and dealt with all the inevitable difficulties. Raffi had left a note propped up against the mirror above the washbasin. It said simply -

"I'm sorry. Please please forgive me. I can't take the nightmares, night after night, any more. I am going to join mother. I love you all. Raffi."

Garabed Asadourian, an Armenian from the central Anatolian town of Kayseri, had had two sons and several daughters. One of the first of the prominent Armenians to have been arrested in April 1915, he had survived the ethnic cleansing, the deportations and massacres of Armenians which went on for about a year after that April. However, his wife and daughters had all been murdered or had collapsed and died on the death marches of that year. The only female in the family to have survived was the little girl – Satenig – currently in the soothing arms of Ara. She had survived only because as a baby, abandoned under the body of her mother, who had shielded her from the bullets as she died, she had been found and brought up by a Turkish woman. This was a good woman whose compassion and religion meant more to her than the fanatic nationalist propaganda of the Ittihad government of the time.

Vahan was eighteen in the summer of 1914 when war broke out in Europe. He had gained a scholarship to attend University and had arrived in the capital in July, four weeks after the fatal shots had been fired in Sarajevo, just as the final countdown to war began. Four months later, in November of that year, the Ottoman Empire had taken the fatal decision to join the war, and by doing so had turned a basically European war into a true World War.

By virtue of his position as a student in the prestigious University, Vahan had automatically become an officer in the Ottoman army and had started military training at the Harbiye. Throughout the war he had remained in Constantinople and, as a result, had not directly witnessed the massacres and killings of his people throughout Eastern Anatolia. He had known what had been going on, the terrible extent of the ethnic cleansing visited both on the hapless Armenian farmers of the countryside and merchants of the cities. He had survived the horrors of the time unscathed, in direct contrast to the experience of his younger brother Raffi. Raffi had been sixteen at the time of his father's arrest, and fled from the family home, living alone and in fear for the duration of the war.

After many misadventures, Garabed had arrived in Constantinople together with a young boy – Ara – who he had taken under his care. Garabed had picked up the boy, starving and alone, while they were both fleeing through the wilds of Eastern Anatolia. Ara had witnessed the bloody deaths of his parents and all his brothers and sisters. On his own and traumatised, he would not have survived had Garabed not found and looked after him. Garabed had been caught up right from the start in the middle of these terrible and terrifying events, events which were to be considered as the first deliberate and violent ethnic cleansing of the twentieth century; a century which was to witness so many more.

But Vahan, like most of the prosperous Armenian community in Constantinople, had seen nothing of all this. Aware of the embassies of their Allies, the Ittihad government made sure that similar outrages were not seen in the capital. So it was that the bloody sight in the bathroom affected him far more than Ara or Garabed, both of whom had put up with sights far worse, during those two years of 1915 and 1916. It was Garabed who saw to all the purely practical details with the help of Ara, while Vahan remained in a daze for some time. When, on that terrible day, Vahan finally got back to his room, which was across the corridor on the same floor as the bathroom and Raffi's bedroom, he found, propped up on the mantelpiece above the fireplace a bulky envelope which he had not noticed when first going to the bathroom that morning. It was in Raffi's handwriting and it was addressed to him. He realised

that Raffi must have crept into his room sometime during the night – perhaps looked down at
him as he slept – before leaving the letter, leaving
the room and leaving this life. Every word of the
letter would remain seared into Vahan's mind for
the rest of his life.

Chapter 2

The birth of Conrad

Conrad Bridgeman was born the year before the death of Raffi Asadourian in the summer of 1923 on the very day that the Treaty of Lausanne was signed by the Greek and Turkish governments in the ugliest building in the whole of Switzerland – the Chateau d'Ouchy on the banks of the Lac du Geneve. However, neither Conrad himself nor his mother Olga Bridgeman, were the slightest bit interested in the event taking place in that building, which an American reporter at the time described as making any Town Hall in the most provincial city in the Midwest look like the Parthenon. They were both far too busy – one pushing and sweating and groaning – the other waiting patiently to come out into the world.

Conrad's father, Harry, was marginally more interested in the news coming out of Lausanne as he waited in the room set aside in the nativity clinic for nervously expectant fathers. This was 1923, there was absolutely no question of mere fathers being allowed to witness the mysteries of childbirth. Harry, however, was not in the slightest bit nervous as it happens. He had always been able to compartmentalise events and feelings in his life, enabling him to think simultaneously of one matter when he was with one person, and a completely different problem when he was with another. He was standing alongside his father, Colonel William Bridgeman who was seated comfortably in an easy chair waiting there in support of his son. Harry was able to be both in total empathy with Olga's ordeal in the next room, while at the same time conversing about extraneous matters with his father without any feeling of disorientation.

The minutes in the waiting-room ticked by.

"Harry, my boy, have you heard that that wily old bird Lord Curzon has pulled it off and the Greeks and the new Turkish nationalists are at this very moment finally putting pen to paper in Lausanne."

"What are you talking about, father.?"

"The Lausanne conference – the Lausanne conference. They've been at it for over six months and most of the negotiations were about the refugees from Smyrna where you yourself were last year."

"Ah yes, sorry, now I'm with you."

Harry, by now an increasingly senior Naval Officer despite having had to face a court-martial only the year before, had been in command of a Royal Navy warship in the bay of Smyrna at the moment of the dramatic burning of that city in September. The Turkish nationalist army had stormed into the city in the wake of the retreating Greek army as it had fled in undisciplined panic desperate to get on to boats taking them out of Anatolia. Harry had had the temerity to disobey orders issued by the British Admiral in command of the fleet forbidding all Captains to pick up any drowning citizens of the city struggling in the waters. These were the increasingly frantic civilians who had been pushed or jumped into the water as the relentless fire approached the quayside to where most of the population had fled. He had been court-martialled before a military court sitting in the old Harbiye building in Constantinople, the capital of the now defunct Ottoman Empire.

Harry had been fairly convinced of his moral position. Supported as he had been by his father, who had travelled out to the city to be with him, he had always been clear in his mind that he would have been unable to live with his conscience if he had not acted as he did. The Greek, Armenian and Jewish quarters of the city had burnt to the ground before his horrified eyes and those of his young officers and men. By that time, he had already been in the Service over ten years and he had remained calm and professional throughout. Nevertheless, his action in picking up an exhausted fifteen-year old girl who was clearly drowning was in plain breach of the orders issued by the British Admiral. This young girl, having been denied access to the British flagship – the HMS Iron Duke – had swum away and was about to go under for ever as she approached Harry's ship. One of the British sailors instinctively jumped overboard to save her, and both were carefully hauled back on board. Harry had compounded his disobedience by then picking up a further hundred or so citizens of Ottoman Smyrna floundering in the bay and clearly about to die.

The fact that the British Admiral in command – Sir Osmond de Beauvoir Brock – faced by murmurings amongst his own men later relented, reversed his orders and even sent out his own boats like the French and Italians had been doing for hours, was no excuse.

The case had been well argued, but in the end no tribunal would have found against a senior admiral of the Royal Navy, and Harry had been duly found guilty. He had been sentenced to a minor loss of seniority and an official reprimand. It was probably the mildest punishment he could have been given and he had accepted it without any rancour or bitterness. He had, however, lost command of his own ship and was now back in London working at the Admiralty in his old job of Naval Intelligence.

Harry turned to focus on his father, sitting at his side, to continue the conversation, when a stiffly starched nurse came into the room and reported that Olga was doing well. She tried to explain that the waters had broken, but as this was a first baby they expected it would be sometime yet before the baby was born. Harry had no idea what she was talking about and nor for that matter did the old Colonel. This was a time when men like Harry and William neither knew nor wanted to know anything about the mysteries of childbirth. They stared at her and nodded. She gave a little smile and went out again.

"So father, tell me what is it that they have actually finally decided at Lausanne about all the refugees and about Greco-Turkish relations as a whole,"

It had been those terrible events in Smyrna and his return to the devastated city a few days after the fire had finally died out, which had so changed Harry's life. Suspended pending the court-martial, Harry had managed to return to help in the evacuation of the quarter of a million desperate souls crowding on the quayside with nowhere to go and with the still-smouldering ashes of the town behind them. It was there that he had found a wife. It was also as a result of his experiences there and the subsequent court-martial that he had entered into a completely new and close relationship with his father. This had resulted in a warm bond between them which had enriched both their lives.

Old Colonel William had travelled to Constantinople in difficult circumstances in order to support his son. There, entranced by the magic of the city and with the help of the Avakian family who were to become his in-laws, father and son had enjoyed the time spent together. Like so many fathers and sons in early 20th century England, they might otherwise have ended up unknown to each other and missed out on the warmth and love they were able to extend each other.

Harry looked at his father and repeated the question.

"Ah yes, well, considering the difficulty we

were in, Curzon did pretty well. We have to evacuate Constantinople almost immediately. However, we have kept control of Mosul which becomes part of the new country - Iraq. The Turkish republic takes over Eastern Thrace, but Greece retains Western Thrace. Ironically, considering all the blood spent over nearly ten years, these Thracian frontiers are the same frontiers as existed before the War began. But the big change, the really exciting part, is that there is to be an agreed exchange of populations. All the Greeks living in Anatolia, including of course those that you helped to evacuate from Smyrna, will have to go and live in Greece. At the same time, all those Turks who live in Crete and in Western Thrace must leave and go and live in the new Turkey. I believe it's in the region of a million or so on each side. Seems to me to be a good solution for a longstanding problem."

"But father, these people, both communities, have each lived in these areas for centuries. Good heavens, the so-called Turks living in Crete speak only Greek, whilst apart from the Smyrniotes who have already been forced out anyway, the Greeks who live in Anatolia speak only Turkish. It sounds terrible! They will have to leave their fields, their neighbours and the farms which they have tended lovingly for centuries and go and live amongst strangers."

"Nonsense my boy – they've been at each other's throats for centuries. This way we will have real peace in the area for once."

"But father that is just a myth created by nationalist leaders on both sides. The two communities have had to live together under the multi-national Ottoman Empire for centuries. They may not have been great buddies, but on the whole they rubbed along together fairly comfortably. Exchange of populations sounds innocuous but it is a terrible precedent. It must be the most blatant exercise of the power of the state over its individual citizens that I have ever come across. I really do hope that it is not going to end up being the norm for the coming century."

But William was not going to agree. He had not witnessed the trauma of thousand upon thousands of uncomprehending families having to abandon homes lived in for generations as had Harry. The esoteric discussion, fairly irrelevant in the circumstances, rambled on until Conrad finally emerged into the world in the next room and began bawling, causing the two men to stop immediately and turn their attention to the door. They were both finally let into the bedroom once Conrad had been cleaned up and Olga too made to look coy and sweet propped up on pristine white pillows. This was 1923 and men were not expected or indeed allowed to be a witness to the messier parts of the arrival of their offspring.

Conrad, half Armenian and half English was to become Vahan's nephew, that is if Vahan could ever get round to persuading Nerissa, his current love and Olga's younger sister, to marry him.

Chapter 3

Nerissa

Nerissa Avakian, Olga's younger sister was a serious soul. She neither had the calm certainty of superiority that Sima, the eldest of the Avakian girls, possessed, nor the outstanding beauty and elegance of Olga nor for that matter the childish charm and ebullience of the youngest of the sisters Seta, who was still not yet sixteen. But she was much the most intelligent of the four girls. She was fluent in four languages - English, French, Armenian and Turkish and was competent in Italian as well. She read avidly and was particularly fond of the English romantic novelists of the nineteenth century.

Her father, Karekin, given the prejudices of early twentieth century Constantinople, had had eccentrically liberal views about the education of women. He also believed in the right, indeed the duty, of everybody including children to discuss and question everything. The more eccentric the doubt, or the more outrageous the questioning, the more he liked it. So Nerissa had been brought up to discuss everything openly and to go fearlessly, and without inhibitions, wherever her logic took her. She was encouraged, as were all the children, to consider all sides of an argument though always remaining polite and tolerant of other peoples points of view.

This was of course all very well when it was within the family, used as they were to the same bold intellectual quest for the truth. But once outside the family circle she had come across many people, indeed probably the majority, for whom many matters, many beliefs, were deeply and emotionally held and not subject to rational or coldly logical debate. In these circumstances, Nerissa would become oddly embarrassed by what she somewhat arrogantly thought of as their stupidity. She expected everyone to argue their case with conviction certainly, but dispassionately. She found that if and when anger or passion arose and logic was thrown out of the window, she could not cope with the emotion displayed, and she would dry up.

Vahan, like Harry, had been a close friend of the Avakian family. The end of the Great War had brought a significant lessening of the formalities of society in Constantinople. Vahan and Nerissa had discovered a mutual interest in American Jazz and American-style dancing which had swept the Greek and Armenian youth of the city. It had even extended its influence to some Turks. Indeed Mustapha Kemal himself was an aficionado of the twenties dance floor, and was known to have patronised the dance halls on the Pera and Galata side of the city during the period he was there. Vahan and Nerissa began regularly going out together in the more relaxed atmosphere of the period even while Nerissa was still at university. Vahan worked with his father in the family business and had become not only proficient, but also well-liked by his many business colleagues. Raffi had joined the firm when he had finally arrived back from the killing fields of Anatolia, but he had been unable to settle down and had been erratic in his judgements.

For Nerissa the calm detachment of Vahan and his dispassionate nature made him an ideal companion. He gave her a good time. He was able and indeed willing to keep up with her questing mind, and gave as good as he got in their animated arguments. Above all he was a completely dependable escort. But she harboured no romantic thoughts of any kind. It was as if romance existed only in books. She was totally unaware that Vahan was falling ever deeper in love with her. In many ways, despite the intellect and her freedom of thought, Nerissa was naïve.

At this time, a year or two after the end of the war, Vahan had discovered that his mother's baby daughter was still alive, despite the death of all the of the family's womenfolk during 1915. Vahan had gone to collect her from the Turkish family who had found and looked after her after the slaughter of her mother. It had been dramatic and difficult enough tearing the little girl away from the only family she had ever known up to then, but transforming the Turkish Rehia, for that was the only name she knew, into the Armenian Satenig, the name given to her at birth by her own mother, was an even longer and more difficult process. It was in this process that Nerissa had been so helpful to the now all-male Asa-dourian family.

Vahan had fallen head over heels in love with Nerissa long before she herself realised the effect she had on the young man. For her, the stolid sensible Vahan was only a companion. Where was the great love that would sweep her off her feet she was so fond of reading about? At one stage, she even imagined herself to be falling for Raffi's dark, sultry and brooding good looks, his face perpetually ravaged by an inner despair she could never fathom. But he was fairly brusque with her, as he was with everyone, and she soon emerged from that rather fanciful infatuation. That, however, caused a sort of rebound and at last, the sheer persistence of Vahan took effect. She did not think that this was the 'lurv' of any nineteenth-century novel she had imagined, but it was certainly something more than just affection on her part. She accepted him.

Karekin Avakian, one of the best-known merchants of the city had already married off his two elder daughters. Sima, his eldest, had fallen in love with a penniless young White Russian aristocrat who had arrived in Constantinople with the remnants of General Wrangel's defeated White army when they evacuated the Crimea from the port of Sevastopol. Their marriage and hasty departure to Italy had been low-key. Olga and Harry, the parents of the newly-born Conrad, had married in the old and grand British Embassy – now only a consulate situated half-way along the

Grande Rue de Pera, and here again Karekin had not been able to be lavish. The marriage of Nerissa to another merchant family of the city gave him the excuse, at last, to splash out. So Vahan and Nerissa had had a traditional Stambuli wedding, celebrated at Tokatlians with all the pomp and trimmings that Karekin had been unable to bestow on the weddings of his first two daughters.

Nerissa believed that something might end up missing in her marriage. What it would be she was not sure – some joy – some chemical spark perhaps. Within only a week or two she knew she had been completely wrong. Vahan might be a bit stolid and a touch unimaginative – but he was a kind and considerate lover and Nerissa came to know real love.

However, it soon became apparent that something was indeed missing in the marriage. Both of them were desperately hoping for children, but as the years passed and no children appeared, they began seeking medical advice. The medical consensus was that Nerissa was never likely to be able to conceive. Both of them wanted children and neither of them had any problem with adoption, if it could be arranged.

The Armenian community left in Istanbul, numbering about one hundred thousand, was the only substantial Ottoman Armenian community that had survived the deportations and massacres of the 1915-16 period during which over a million people perished in the first of the twentieth century 'ethnic cleansings'. The city population had many individuals and indeed whole families who had managed to struggle back from the killing fields of the Anatolian mountains, and their fears and prejudices were having an effect on attitudes as a whole. Time and again mothers, having to leave their homes without any of their men to help for what turned out to be death marches, had left their babies with friendly Turkish neighbours. These neighbours were ordinary good people who had refused to be intimidated by the rantings of the exclusive nation-state fanatics of the dominant Ittihad party, backed up by the academics, which had taken root during those dying days of the old Ottoman Empire. People may or may not individually hate their neighbours for all sorts of rational or irrational reasons, but hating a whole community is inevitably a matter of state or religious manipulation. Many Turks, good Moslems most of them, did not fall for the nationalist propaganda, and there were countless examples of such people taking in and looking after babies and children who would otherwise undoubtedly have died.

But all this had resulted in a collective fear in what was left of the Armenian community and a deep irrational prejudice about the adoption of orphans. As so much adoption had been forced on an unwilling people, voluntary adoption had become psychologically fraught. Somehow there was a preference to placing orphans into institutions, often under-funded and understaffed, rather than putting them into the hands of rich childless American-Armenians seeking babies.

This prejudice or fear confronted Vahan and Nerissa and was at its worst just as they first became interested in looking for an orphaned or disadvantaged child for adoption. If they had persevered, there seems to be little doubt that sooner or later an Armenian child seeking surrogate parents would have been found. However, neither wanted to adopt a child over two years-old, at the very most. They were both conditioned by their shared experience in the raising of Satenig. They wanted a baby who would know only them as parents. There were no such Armenian babies anymore.

Chapter 4

As it turned out

Both Billy and his elder sister Natalie were fair-haired and had blue-green eyes. Their mother, Olga Bridgeman, was Armenian, born in Constantinople at the turn of the century. She had a fair complexion with the usual large brown eyes. Their father Harry had blue eyes and light brown hair. It was therefore rather unusual that Conrad, nine years older than Billy, had jet-black hair and black smouldering eyes. However his dark looks belied his friendly character. He was patient and gentle, both with his younger sister Natalie and even more so with his younger brother. Despite the great difference in their ages he would always let the little boy play with his things and leaf clumsily through his books to find whatever pictures took his fancy. If Billy stumbled and fell, it was more often than not his elder brother who would pick him up and cuddle him, washing away the tears.

From fairly early on in their lives the children got used to travelling every summer to spend their summer holidays with their grandparents in Constantinople. Except for the years when a baby was born, and the grandparents came to England for the christening, it was a regular summer ritual, the actual timing depending on school holidays and Harry's work.

Olga's mother and father – Karekin and Armineh Avakian – lived in a large house in a suburb of Istanbul, Makrikoy, about twenty minutes by train from the centre. The Bridgeman family always travelled out on the Simplon-Orient Express. Before Billy was born, they usually went as a family with the parents in one compartment, and Conrad and Natalie in the one next door with a tiny bathroom in between. After Billy was born it would more often be Olga and Natalie in one compartment and the two boys in the other, while Harry, increasingly busy at the Admiralty would come out on his own later.

The coach on which they travelled began at Victoria station, and was part of the daily service known as the Golden Arrow which left for Paris at 10 p.m. every evening. The whole train would be shunted onto the ferry at Dover and shunted off at Calais. After one occasion when Billy, only four years-old, had screamed with anger at having slept through the whole procedure, Conrad would thereafter gently wake him up as the train was shunted onto the ship. The two boys would then peek out from under the green blinds as the train carefully backed onto the rails in the ship. That was enough for Billy and he would be asleep by the time of their arrival in France.

That first breakfast in the train, as it trundled through the flat northern French plains, was always magical. A full English breakfast with all the trimmings would be served as they watched the countryside rushing by. It was not only the joy of eating a meal on a moving train, it was also the only time any of the children ate such a served breakfast like that. Olga had strong reservations about greasy fried bacon and eggs and all that went with it. It was a bone of contention between her and Harry all their lives. Breakfasts at home were always fruit and yoghurt, perhaps some porridge and at most a slice of toast.

On occasional Sundays, however, when Olga remained in bed, she would be joined by Natalie, who crept into her bed and dozed with her after Harry had gone down. Conrad would creep down with Harry and they would cook up an enormous and rather messy breakfast with all sorts of goodies all mixed up together into a great greasy scrambled egg tomato and bacon omelette. Billy would wait eagerly at the table as this culinary extravagance was prepared. Despite every effort in later life, faithfully to copy everything they had done, he had never been able to recreate the taste of that food as a grinning Conrad placed it before him.

All three fondly believed that Olga had no idea what they were doing, but she was perfectly well aware of what went on, even though Conrad carefully tidied and washed up before she came down.

When the train reached Paris, Conrad and Harry would get out at the Gare du Nord. Olga, Natalie and Billy would remain in the coach as it was shunted round the Paris 'ceinture' going forwards and backwards and taking what seemed to be hours and hours. Finally it would arrive at the Gare de Lyons and would be attached with one final lurch to the Simplon-Orient Express waiting there to leave. On those occasions that Harry came with them while Billy was a baby, he and Conrad would join them back on the train, having eaten together at the wonderful Art Deco restaurant in the station.

The train would depart with a lot of fuss, whistles and waving relatives. It raced on through the night into Switzerland, a short stop in Lausanne, and then through the Alps, arriving as the sun was rising into Domodossola. It was always the same, the shouts of "Panini, Birra, Arangiata" from the boys running up and down the platform with their trays, heralding their arrival into the Mediterranean world, followed by the short early morning ride into Milan.

After leaving Trieste, as the train went through the Balkans, sometimes the coach would be separated from all the other blue coaches of the *Compagnie Internationale des Wagon-Lits et des Grands Express Européenes* and, in order to get to the dining car, the family would have to pass through the third-class wooden coaches of the Yugoslav state railways.

This would change at the border after the train entered Bulgaria. The Yugoslav coaches would be abandoned and left on the Yugoslav side and Bulgarian state railway coaches would be added as soon as the train moved over the border and into the first station on the Bulgarian side. The

Bulgarian coaches would then be uncoupled before the train moved into Turkey. By the time the train steamed into Sirkedji station – the terminus and the end of the line in what was now Istanbul – it was again the original train that had set out from Paris three days before. As the train passed through Makrikoy it was always the family ritual that Olga would excitedly point out the little station from which she had gone to school every day before the War. About a quarter of an hour later, the train would pass through the great walls of the old city and, skirting round the Topkapi Palace grounds, would arrive with a great deal of hissing, steaming, whistles and excitement alongside Platform 1 of Sirkedji station.

Here, summer after summer, the Bridgemans would be welcomed by the whole of the extended family. Everyone with any relationship at all – the Avakians – the Asadourians – and a host of others would be on the platform to welcome the British branch of the family.

Karekin Avakian, Olga's father and Conrad's grandfather, would stand in front of the large mirror in his bedroom every morning for a few moments looking into his own eyes and carefully adjusting his grey tie, even though it was already impeccably correct. He would always make a final check to make sure that his well-cut grey suit was perfect to the last button. Karekin was over six feet tall, unusually tall for an Armenian from the city of Istanbul. In public, he would stand ramrod stiff with his hands almost invariably behind him and resting in the small of his back. He had remained a well-known and influential figure in the city not only amongst the Armenians but amongst all the merchant communities.

The city itself – still Polis for the Greeks and Bolis to the Armenians – had of course lost its great prestige and influence. From its status as the great Imperial capital of three different Empires over 1500 years, it had now ceased to be a capital at all. The Embassies had all moved to the unutterably boring new city of Ankara plumb in the middle of a remote part of Anatolia. The name of Constantinople had ceased to exist, and it had become Istanbul – the second city of a new Republic.

However, despite its relegation, it continued to contain a vibrant and varied population, although non-Turks were no longer in the majority. This mixed culture, so important an element in the old Ottoman world, had been saved by an agreed exception to the draconian exchange of populations imposed by the Treaty of Lausanne. This had allowed the Greeks, Armenians, other Christians and Jews of the ancient city to be excepted from the articles of 'ethnic cleansing' so admired by the politicians and academics of the time.

Karekin himself had survived his arrest in April 1915 and the terrible slaughter that had accompanied the deportations of Armenians during that year. On his return at the end of the War, he had reopened his merchant house – largely based on the importation of Lancashire muslins. He had thrived, as had most of Constantinople, during the four years of the British occupation. But the collapse of the Greek army in September 1922 followed by the terrible burning of Smyrna and the loss of his only son – Haik – in that great conflagration had aged him and affected his natural optimism. In the end, he had burned the terrifying letter he had received explaining the true circumstances of his son's death, and what had happened to his daughter – Olga – during that same fire. His deliberate burning of that letter had saved his soul and had reconciled him to the need to forgive, if not forget. Coupled to the practical good sense of his wife – Armineh – this had saved him from the worst effects of that most difficult of all guilts – the guilt of the survivor of the sort of catastrophe that had overwhelmed the Armenian people in 1915.

The Avakian house was large and set at the front of a substantial walled garden with orchards and woods at the far end. It stood directly on the road leading down the hill to the Cobancesme railway station. The house was now far too large for what remained of the family.

Karekin's son, Haik, had been the fourth of his children. Now left in the house was his last daughter, Seta, still unmarried, together with an adopted boy. This boy, also named Haik, was a refugee orphan from that same terrible fire in Smyrna.

The merchant house of 'Avakian et fils' retained its name although in fact there was now
no 'fils'. If his son Haik had survived, he would of
course have been brought in as a full partner. But
that great fire of Smyrna in September 1922 had
put an end to that. So it was that he remained
alone in his business and inevitably his old-established firm, respected and known throughout the
old Ottoman world, began to decline.

The elderly Garabed Asadourian, on the other
hand, a provincial from Central Anatolia, who
had only arrived in Constantinople as a survivor
of the massacres of 1915 -16, understood well the
art of delegation. Above all, he had two sons – Vahan and Ara – both alive and ready to take over
many aspects of the firm's business, including the
vital need to expand and initiate new developments. Accordingly, 'Asadourian et fils', thrived
and began to dominate the textile and carpet
houses of the city's commercial sector.

At the same time, the old-established firm of
Avakian & Co. faltered and fell back month by
month from its old pre-eminent position in the
commercial world of the city. This was caused
largely by the increasing failure of Lancashire
goods to compete in the world markets and was
exacerbated by the lack of any young male or
even female junior partner to bolster the increasingly world-weary efforts of Karekin.

The little boy, saved from those same flames of
Smyrna that caused the death of Karekin's own
son, was supposed to have taken over the role of

the next son in the family. But it soon became clear that he would not be taking over or even joining the family firm. He had a dreamy somewhat effeminate character, crying easily and lacking any competitive drive. He was a great favourite of Armineh who had doted on him as a sort of antidote to the grief she still felt for her own son, who had died when he was only 19. She herself was now in her sixties and had indulged the child in a way she would never have done with any of her own children. Fortunately the lad had a natural sweetness and diffidence of character which had prevented him from simply turning into a 'spoilt child'.

The little Armenian school in Makrikoy had closed and Haik, had gone to the newly reopened English High School in the city. This entailed daily commuting on the line from Cobancesme to Sirkedji. He found it difficult and a bit daunting at first. His command of English, no longer much spoken in the house after the departure of the three girls, was not good. Everything conspired to reduce his confidence and self-esteem. Even his nickname "Yegrort Haik" – second Haik – constantly reminded him of his position in the Avakian household.

It goes without saying that neither Karekin nor Armineh ever said 'Yegrort Haik' nor allowed any of the servants to repeat it. But nonetheless, the nickname had stuck, and everyone except the close family used it without thinking. Seta, the youngest of the Avakian girls, was already in her late twenties when he stumbled into puberty at the age of 14. She too had been over-protective towards the little boy, and like Armineh had been unable to change as Haik turned from being a boy of 12 into the youth of 14.

And what of Karekin? He should have been the one to stiffen the boy's resolve and help him through puberty and into adolescence. But Karekin never faced up to it. It always preyed on his mind that on the very day that his own son Haik had been assaulted near the house as a young boy, he had been arrested in the city and deported. At that very traumatic moment, when the boy had needed a father more than at any other time in his life, Karekin had disappeared and could not re-enter his son's life until the crisis had passed and his son had moved into adolescence and young adulthood. The fact that it had not had any lasting effect on his son, nor that he could have avoided this absence, was immaterial to his feelings of guilt. He had not been there when his only son had so badly needed strong male reassurance. Somehow, as a result, he had been unable to extend to this boy, an adopted son the help and advice that he had failed to extend to his own son.

Chapter 5

Joshua Benussan

At its height and right up to the 17th century, the Ottoman Empire was one of the most tolerant of the major states of Europe and the Near East. Whilst Islam was the state religion, thus making non-believers second-class citizens, it also tolerated the other religions of 'the book'. Judaism was acceptable, as were the various Christian sects. When the Spanish Empire expelled the large community of Sephardic Jews from the whole of Spain, the Ottoman state was the only state in Europe prepared to accept them and allow them to settle.

By comparison, the French state, for example, revoked the Edict of Nantes and expelled the French Protestants numbering many thousands, all of whom had to flee and settle in various other countries dotted about Northern Europe. Some of them even made their way to the Ottoman East. Even England – a byword in its own opinion for tolerance – made life extremely difficult for Catholics, who could not vote, enter Parliament or hold any official post. This was all in stark contrast to the Ottoman Empire where Greeks, for example, could and did become diplomats of the Empire, representing the Ottomans in many European conferences. Albanians and Egyptians became Chief Viziers. Armenians were often chosen as state architects and controlled and managed many banks.

So it was that there was a large Jewish population throughout the Empire. The wealthiest and largest community of Jews were the prosperous descendents of the large Sephardic community thrown out of Catholic Spain. The Ottoman Sultan had given them sanctuary, when no other European power had been prepared to do so. They had prospered to the point that they had become the largest ethnic group in Salonica, which was the second port of the Empire in Europe. There was also a large and again prosperous community of Jews in Smyrna, which was the second port of the Empire in Asia. Ironically, where those communities were wealthy and highly regarded, the Jews of Constantinople, the Empire's premier port for both continents, were poor and without influence. There was no specific Jewish quarter such as there was in Smyrna, though most Jews lived along the shores of the Golden Horn in the rather drab areas of Stamboul lying between the end of the Galata bridge and Eyub.

There was no official anti-Semitism in the Ottoman state, and certainly the Salonica Sephardic community was highly respected and usually had good relations with the Ottoman governors. But for some reason Constantinople itself was different. Some officials caused difficulties and purported to despise the Jews despite state policy. Sometimes some of the Christians in the capital – admittedly the more ignorant minority – could be even worse than the Turkish bureaucrats, though there was never any violence.

After the war, when more stable conditions arose all over Europe, Garabed's business boomed. Although the many Armenian families from whom he had commissioned carpets before the War had disappeared in the deportations and the massacres, he had made new contacts with Kurdish and Iranian families who produced the same fine products. He sold these all over the world, but particularly to the grand carpet houses of London and Paris. His son Vahan, who had originally come to the business reluctantly, had proved to have a sharp commercial sense. He also soon became known as being very fair in his dealings and to be scrupulously honest. Using an American phraseology, he would often say to his staff – "Try to make sure that the other guy goes away as happy with the deal as you are." He was, as a result, respected and liked in the commercial circles of the city.

Garabed tried to have no racial distinctions in his employment policy. Inevitably the business started with a preponderance of Armenian employees, but as the business expanded there were many Greeks and Jews as well as Armenians working in various different departments throughout the company. The time would come when the fact that there were no Turks would cause him some distress – but now in the twenties it caused no problem.

One of his employees who worked in the Accounts department was a hard-working young man whose name was Joshua Benussan. Joshua had been brought up in a Jewish orphanage where he had originally been deposited as a foundling baby. That year a wealthy Salonica merchant – Benussan – had made a substantial charitable donation to the Constantinople orphanage. Several of the boys without names taken in during that year were given his surname out of respect. Joshua's wife Rachel had also been at the same orphanage. She had given birth to a little boy soon after they were married, whom they had named Hakim – more of a Turkish name than a more traditional Jewish one. However, they were both assiduous attendees at their local synagogue and were true and devout believers.

Joshua was cheerful and had a great fund of humourous stories directed at the funnier aspects of his co-religionists. He would regale other members of the staff with these often silly but very funny stories poking fun at Jewish stereotypes. However woe betide any of his gentile colleagues who repeated or produced similar stories themselves. In such cases he would show that he was offended, and as he was a popular figure in the office people were careful to avoid anything of that nature. On the day of a fateful series of events, Vahan had slipped into the Accounting office from a side door which led to his room alone. He needed to find a file which was in the Department's filing cabinet. Unnoticed, he waited to listen, having arrived just as Joshua was in the throes of yet another of his inimitable stories.

"Well, you see, my friends, there was Salomon" – the fictional shabby Salomon was often the butt of Joshua's stories – "really tired out and still far from home in the middle of this hot day. Deciding he could go no further for the moment, he flopped down on the pavement by the side of the road and leant back where there was a bit of shade against a wall. The heat and all that food worked on him and soon he fell fast asleep. There he was, snoring away, when who should come sauntering by but Achmet." His audience, including Vahan in the corner, chuckled, for Achmet too was a well-loved favourite in Joshua's stories – the rather stupid local Turkish policeman.

"Anyway, my friends, Achmet took one look and gave the hapless Salomon a great kick. Then he took his truncheon and gave him a blow across his shoulder, shouting - 'wake up Jew – wake up, you can't lie there like a dog'. Salomon had woken up with the kick and had opened his eye to stare at his old enemy. The blow with the truncheon brought him fully awake staring at Achmet's ugly visage grinning down at him'. He sat up and started crying out –

'Ach! Ach! Woe is me, Oh dear. Oh dear. Effendi – he's still there – he's still there.'

'What the devil are you talking about,' says Achmet, prodding poor Salomon again with his baton.

'Oh dear! Oh dear! I daren't tell you. You'll beat me again if you knew what you had done.' He continued wailing like this despite all Achmet could do to get him to tell. Well my friends you can imagine that Achmet was now very curious. He says, 'Look you better tell me. I promise I won't beat you – but I certainly will if you don't.'

"Well effendi it's like this. While I was asleep I dreamt that I was in heaven. There sat God on his throne. Behind him stood Moses, and to one side was Jesus, and on the other, naturally the honourable right-hand side, stood Mohammed. Anyway, while I was there one of God's slippers fell off, and oh dear, policeman bey, it fell right down to the other place far below. 'Who will go and fetch it for me' says God. Well Achmet bey you know what a coward Moses is, and he shook his head. God turned to Jesus, but you know how lazy he is and he too shook his head. But Mohammed – well you know how brave and generous he is, he immediately said he would go down and bring it back. So I saw him bravely going down to hell – but then, Oh dear, Oh dear! just as he reached the bottom you woke me up and he's still there!"

At this point Salomon got up and walked off – leaving poor Achmet standing trying to work out what had happened and whether it was his fault."

There were broad grins and chuckles round the office, but then they saw Vahan who had moved to the filing cabinet to pick up his file. They scuttled back to their desks. Vahan was known to disapprove of this sort of joke. He never had much sense of humour in any case, but he particularly disliked jokes which relied on national or religious stereotypes. They all knew that he was not a believer, so they were always surprised when he showed his objection to this kind of joke. But, however silly he thought some of these religious beliefs were, he felt it was wrong and dangerous to poke fun at them. Picking up his file he walked out saying –

"Could you please come to my office, Joshua."

Once Joshua arrived and sat down, Vahan did not mince his words –

" Joshua, I don't want to be heavy-handed, but I must insist that you put an end to all these stories. You only get away with it because we have no Turkish employees at the moment. But we may have some in the future and I am not happy about it in any case. I should add that I am also just as unhappy about the jokes you make about Jews. Jokes of this kind are the thin edge of the wedge. I would also ask you to think about the fact that in the huge fund of Turkish humourous stories about their figure of fun Nasreddin Hodja, there are never any jibes poked at Christians or Jews."

" I am truly sorry, sir. I have never meant any harm."

"Well, yes, I know that – I would not be having this conversation at all if I thought for a moment that there was any malice in your stories,"

"It is only my way of keeping cheerful despite the many problems I have."

"What problems? Do we not pay you enough?"

"Yes Vahan bey – the house has always been

generous. But I have a two year-old baby, and my wife is not very well and…."

"Well, if there is anything I can do I will. But Joshua, I cannot increase your wages. If I did I would have to raise everyone else as well."

"I accept that, sir, and I did not raise the matter in order to try and get a rise, but I have heard you talking with the lady Nerissa hanum, and have heard her mentioning to you that she was thinking of getting a new cook."

"Yes…well,"

"My wife is a good cook, sir, and it would be very helpful to my family if Mdme Asadourian might consider interviewing her for the job."

"Hm – I don't see why not. What about the baby? Oh well never mind, no doubt your wife will make her own arrangements. Listen, I will take no responsibility. Tell your wife to call on Mdme Asadourian tomorrow. But remember I promise nothing – it will depend on the ladies. Meanwhile Joshua please try to make your stories more innocuous."

Chapter 6

Rachel

Rachel Benussan was not as joyful and cheerful as her husband Joshua. She had known Joshua for almost the whole of her life. They were both orphans, and both had been brought up in the same rather shabby and run-down orphanage situated in a poor quarter of Stamboul. Both she and Joshua had been brought up as orthodox practising Jews, but while Joshua became sceptical, she had never for a moment questioned the beliefs into which she had been inculcated as a child. Rachel had hated her life in the orphanage, as indeed had Joshua, but while Joshua had turned it all in his mind into a sort of joke, in Rachel's case it had festered into a bitter memory. So it was that when Joshua left the orphanage after he had got his first modest job at the age of sixteen, Rachel had not hesitated for a moment when almost two years later Joshua arrived back at the orphanage and asked her to marry him.

There had been no love or tenderness at the institution where they had both lived. The orphanage was completely dependent on charitable donations almost entirely provided by the wealthy members of the Salonica community. The Guardians had done their best – there was no suggestion of any abuse or cruelty – but a strict regime of religion was no substitute for the care, however messy and incompetent it might be, of a parent.

When Joshua got home from the day of the meeting with Vahan, he burst out –

"Listen my darling, I had a bit of a difficult interview with Mr. Asadourian this afternoon. He was telling me off about something...no...no...it's not important. Never mind about it. Anyway I raised the matter that Mdme Asadourian had said she was looking for another cook. I suggested that you might be given an interview."

"But Joshua, husband..."

"No, listen, we need the extra income and..."

"But Joshua, you listen – that sort of family don't just need a cook for easy family meals. They entertain, and their cook would have to prepare formal meals for a dozen or more guests and I doubt if..."

"Rachel, once you are in, I know you would manage and they would make excellent employers – if of course you get on with her. I've seen her several times in the office and believe me she is not the stuck up sort."

"Oh Joshua you go rushing ahead as always without thinking of all the complications in what you are suggesting. What about Hakim? I simply could not leave him with strangers all day in some awful kindergarten. You know how we both felt about the orphanage."

For once this left Joshua speechless. But he soon bounced back.

"Rachel, my love, I agree with you. I too could

not impose anything like that on our son. But look – take Hakim with you tomorrow and go and see Mdme Asadourian in any case. Who knows?"

So it was that on the very next day Rachel, with her twelve month old baby in her arms, took the ferry from the next stop after Eyub to the quays under the Galata bridge. Then up the Tunel to the station at the top at the start of the Grande Rue de Pera, now renamed Istiklal Caddesi. From there, using the tram, she eventually arrived at the apartment in the area known as Osman Bey where Vahan and Nerissa now lived in a modern apartment block which even had a lift.

From that very first meeting Nerissa and Rachel took to each other. Nerissa was charmed by the dark black-haired beauty of Rachel, and pleased with her serious and warm nature – tempered though it was with a physical frailty that seemed to emanate from her. They both had a similar seriousness of temperament which made them impatient with gossip or small-talk. She agreed to take on Rachel for a trial period of two weeks to see how Rachel managed with her duties. It worked well and on the fifth day Rachel even came out with flying colours in the preparation of a formal evening meal with four guests on a Sunday.

It did not take long for Nerissa to sort out Rachel's main problem – how to deal with the baby. She quickly appreciated that Joshua and Rachel, both orphans brought up without any loving parents or siblings, could not contemplate leaving their son for any length of time to be looked after day after day by strangers. So every day little Hakim accompanied his mother to the grand apartment in Osman Bey where he would play round Rachel's legs in the kitchen as he grew older and became a toddler. Then, as time went on, so long as there were no guests, he slowly began to have the run of the corridors and some rooms – usually with an eye kept on him by the young maids and cleaning ladies employed during the day. On evenings when there were formal guests, Joshua would pick him up after the office and take him home.

The little boy rarely saw Vahan, except on Sundays. Saturday was Rachel's day off, and he would be at home with his parents. From an early age he went with his father to the local synagogue. He had already been circumcised, and from the rather early age of four he began joining in with other children for religious instruction. Nerissa's reaction to the daily presence of the little boy was complex. On the one hand she came to love the child in a rather abstract way. Her main feelings, however, were centred on Rachel who had become a friend as well as the family cook. But there was a tinge of envy which, try as she might, she could not entirely suppress. Her continued failure to have children of her own always disturbed her, although as the years passed and she passed her thirtieth year, she had come to accept it as her lot in life.

Hakim had his fourth birthday with a splendid birthday party in the Osman Bey apartment. Nerissa had invited a Greek neighbour's children of the same age who lived in the apartment below and who occasionally had come up to play with Hakim, whilst Rachel invited some boys from the Synagogue school. For once the event went very well, without the usual tears and tantrums so often the adjunct of this sort of over-the-top adult-inspired children's party. It was at the end of this party, as Joshua, Rachel and Hakim got ready to take the taxi home that Vahan had insisted on ordering, that Rachel with an enormous smile whispered to Nerissa that she was pregnant again, and indeed that she had been for some months already and that she was due in just over four months. Nerissa had noticed nothing. Once again she felt that slight touch of envy – but she recognised it at once as unworthy of her and kissed Rachel fondly and with real pleasure at the news.

Joshua had been ill again recently but had refused to go to a doctor, not wanting to distract attention from Rachel's condition and the coming birth. The Benussans were in heaven. Vahan had offered to arrange a mortgage advance to enable them to move and purchase a better home on the Pera side. Joshua suppressed the pains in his stomach as the great day for the second birth began to loom. Rachel stopped coming to work and Nerissa somewhat reluctantly agreed to look after Hakim once labour started and until Rachel could get up again.

Then – in the midst of all that happiness, trag-edy struck. There was of course no question of a hospital. Rachel was to have her baby at home like everyone else of her class and position. In-deed few people of any class in Constantinople had their babies in hospital at that time. The Jew-ish midwife had been coming and had said that she was a bit concerned due to the rather feverish frailty of her charge. Vahan diffidently suggested that Rachel could perhaps go to a hospital – the Armenian hospital, Sourp Pirgic, was nearby. However no one took him seriously. In the end, complications arose during the birth, which was both painful and premature, and the baby girl emerged stillborn. Rachel herself survived for only a few more hours in great pain and distress before she, too, died.

A few days later at the funeral Joshua col-lapsed suddenly. This time Vahan took over and absolutely insisted that a good doctor – his own family physician, should be called in. The doctor examined him and in turn insisted that Joshua be admitted to hospital immediately. Again Sourp Pirgic was the most convenient and Karekin be-ing a trustee, Nerissa had no difficulty in getting Joshua admitted into a private room immediately. In due course the desperate Joshua, still grieving for the death of his wife and still-born daughter, was diagnosed with cancer of the stomach. All this time, as the Benussan family lurched from one crisis to the next, Nerissa had been looking after Hakim. At Rachel's funeral it was her hand that the little boy held on to desperately as the service droned on.

It would be ill-natured and voyeuristic to describe day by day the agonies of the last days of Joshua Benussan. He was in perpetual pain, but his mind remained sharp and clear. If his fund of funny stories had necessarily dried up, his brain had not. The one thing that both he and Rachel had always agreed on was that they would not allow their son to end up in an institution, another orphanage, to live a life without love. Nerissa, meanwhile, continued looking after the little boy, though she did have help of course. Short of some other institution or a professional of some sort, there really was no one else. She took Hakim at least twice a week to spend some time with his father in the hospital – but it soon became painfully apparent to them both that the little boy was getting confused by everything that had happened in the last few months.

It was fast becoming obvious that Joshua too was dying. On a daily basis he pleaded with Vahan to make sure that his son did not end up in an orphanage. He made it clear, even as he wasted away, that he was desperate to avoid institutionalising his son. He wanted Nerissa to keep looking after the boy. Difficult though it was, as it had to be done quickly while Joshua was still alive, his wishes were all dealt with and completed after only a few weeks. Both Nerissa's father, the highly respected and influential Karekin, and Vahan's father Garabed called in all their contacts and everyone, including officials, owing them obligations. Accordingly in due course, an adoption order of sorts was hurried through. There could not be any name change; there was no change of the original birth certificate. The child's 'nufus' remained unchanged.

Hakim Benussan – now almost five years old – became the legally adopted son of Vahan and Nerissa Asadourian. The 'nufus' (the identity paper) of the new Turkish Republic was not all that different from that of the old Ottoman style. Vahan's nufus had the tell-tale line with the word "Ermeni," as did that of all Armenians. Hakim's nufus, like that of his father and mother also stated in that same line clearly the word "Yahudi".

On the very last day of 1935, Joshua Benussan smiled at his two visitors – Nerissa Asadourian and her son – his son – Hakim Benussan – stretched out his hand, and died.

Chapter 7

Raffi's letter

In the summer of 1936 when Hakim was 5, Garabed decided that the carpet side of the business should be expanded and after talking it over with Vahan, it was decided that he and Nerissa should move to Paris and open a branch of the firm there. It was all a matter of growing trade and commerce. Despite the arrival in Germany of Hitler and the Nazi Party no one was for the moment concerned about the possibility of another war. Hadn't the Great War been fought as a war to end all wars? The British navy was still the undisputed master of the seas and the French army was the largest and strongest in Europe. Democracy may have been dying in Eastern Europe – but in the West it remained triumphant. Even Catholic and authoritarian Spain now had a Republican government, a little shaky though it was.

The evening before their departure to France, after Nerissa had gone to bed, Vahan took out Raffi's letter – the letter which he had found propped up on the mantelpiece of his bedroom in the old family house on Osmanli Sokag. More than ten years had passed since the terrible day of his brother's death, and he had read and reread the letter many times since then. It was not that he had brooded inordinately on that day or on the letter itself, but it had always been there at the back of his mind. Vahan could look back on the last ten years with a lot of pleasure and satisfaction. His marriage to Nerissa had been a great success and he remained deeply in love with her. His father, too, had mellowed since Raffi's death and Vahan's relationship with him had improved. Garabed had a strong personality who had seen a good deal more of the seamier and more violent side of life during the last years of the Ottoman Empire than Vahan and had coped with his son's death better than Vahan. He grieved for his second son, obviously, but he had also lost his wife and all but one of his daughters during 1915. He had found a way to live with it and his natural strength and willpower had helped him to deal with the trauma. Perhaps it helped also, that while not being overly pious, he was a believer. Vahan, on the other hand, had not experienced the violence and the hatred that had been directed against his people, and which had been experienced personally by his father and brother.

He sighed and opened the letter to read it once again, though not really needing to, as he knew it almost by heart. The letter was unsigned. Vahan had never shown it to anyone –

My darling brother,
I love you Vahan – Please believe me, I have always loved you. If we have had our differences – if sometimes I have been envious of your success and your intellect and understanding, nevertheless I have always looked up to you even when I pretended not to.

I know that you have usually thought of me as being extroverted and somewhat insensitive. It's true that I have always been a bit direct in my speech, and I have tried in these last years to be forceful and decisive in order to make up for the fear and weakness that I lived with during those awful years after 1915 and until I got back to you and father.

But brother you were not there – you never knew that daily, debilitating fear of death under which those of us who managed to escape lived. To know every moment of your waking hours that many people around you are seeking to kill you – not because of anything you ever did to them, but simply because you belong to a particular race or a particular religion, is something that saps away at your soul and your confidence.

I have told you of the horrors of those days in Kayseri after father was arrested, as the Government slowly tightened the screws against the Armenian population. First it was those of the Gregorian Apostolic faith who had to pack up and leave on foot. Then not much later, when they saw that the European allied embassies were not raising any objections, all the rest of the community – the Protestants and Catholics – were also made to go. I don't need to remind you that it was only the proof you sent us that you were an officer in the army that saved us, for the moment, from those death marches. I have already told you about all these matters.

What I have never explained to you is the daily fear as the town was emptied of all six thousand of its Armenian population save a few. The churches were abandoned. The school was closed and I was forced to witness the hanging in the public square of all my teachers. I have never been able to get the sight of their hanging bodies and protruding tongues out of my mind. Nor can I ever forget the bestial shouts of delight from the crowd pressing round me, and my own shame and humiliation as I said nothing and simply looked down at the floor. By this time, apart from mother and our sisters there were perhaps only about fifty Armenians left in the town. The empty desolate streets around me were incredibly depressing and the atmosphere even affected some Turks, who tended to hurry through our old quarter with their eyes down.

All that was bad enough but I have also never told you about the 'hunting party'. I had to try and make a living and I managed to get a job with one of the Turks who had bought from the Commissioner for Armenian property – for a complete pittance of course – a textile store belonging to one of the departed Armenian merchants. I was still 16 and able to move about and I offered my services to this man who had been an acquaintance of father. He had no idea about textiles or how to run a business, and even at that age I was able to do it for him.

For several weeks I had noted that the square in front of the store was often filled in the late afternoons with a group of about twenty men who would arrive on horseback, clearly after they had been out hunting. They would repair to a large café alongside the store. One day several of these men came to visit my boss – Mehmet Bey. I was sent out to collect some more chairs and place then in the main store and to give orders to the coffee maker to bring round coffee for everyone. Mehmet Bey ordered me to pull across a large velvet curtain that cut off a *tiny section of the store which contained the safe and an office desk, where I sat when I got back.*

Oh God Vahan – if only I had never heard. They didn't know that I was sitting there, although I doubt if they would have minded even if they knew. The 'hunt' on which they had been engaged was the hunting of the old men, women and children of the lines of deportees wandering across the countryside. They outdid each other with descriptions of how they accomplished the killings. They remarked how the older women had tried to protect the young girls by putting them in the middle. I heard one say –'I picked up a really pretty young one today. Her mother tried to interfere and begged me to do anything to her but to leave her little daughter alone. So I did what she asked for – I emptied my gun into her giavour cunt, and then took the girl anyway.'

Oh Vahan, the conversations went on like this for over an hour. Each one of them was proud of what they had been doing, each boasting to each other of their exploits. The memory of that hunting party and my fear that I might be discovered cowering behind that curtain has stayed with me and caused me worse nightmares than the horrors I did actually witness. Somehow, whilst I was fighting to survive, although the fear never left me, the instinct to overcome those fears and survive took over. But now that the danger has passed, the nightmares have returned. I wake up every night in a sweat of terror – I see myself being hunted down night after night...

I can't take any more. I have not slept for months. I am irritable and in a state of nerves all day. You know that I am a believer and I believe that God will pardon me. I will be going to join mother and my slaughtered sisters. I beg your forgiveness Vahan. I love you."

With a final sigh, Vahan began slowly and deliberately to tear the letter into tiny shreds. There were no tears – he had already wept over the letter many times during the past ten years. He went over to the French windows and out onto the balcony. He stood there staring out into the night. There was no moon at all, and he couldn't even see down onto the Bosphorus, usually shimmering in the distance even with the slightest moon. Still acting very slowly and deliberately he let the tiny shreds of paper drift away into the night one by one. It was supposed to be a symbolic gesture. By acting as he did he imagined that all the heartache and trauma that the letter represented would be dissipated. He was about to leave Istanbul – that great Imperial city of 1500 years, perched on the world's most significant waterway and straddling two continents – perhaps for ever. It was, he thought, the right symbolic moment to tear up the past and put it all behind him.

As the last shreds of paper floated away in the night, Vahan thought that it had at last all been exorcised – that it was all now behind him. He smiled as he walked back into the sitting-room. His brain told him that he was now free… but the past does not let go that easily!

Chapter 8

Paris in the thirties

Vahan and Nerissa arrived and settled in
Paris in the aftermath of the Stavisky scandal. Sacha Alexandre Stavisky was a Russian born
Jew who had arrived in the country with his parents as immigrants. A colourful character, who
became known as 'le beau Sacha', he had tried
various jobs and had finally ended up as the manager of a municipal pawnshop. He sold a whole
lot of worthless bonds based on the surety of a
store of emeralds that he claimed belonged to the
former German Empress, but which turned out
to be worthless glass. Surely, only a petty criminal
then. Unfortunately for an already demoralised
Third Republic it was a little more than that. It
soon transpired as the scandal developed that he
had connections with many senior Republican
politicians.

Faced with imminent exposure the handsome
and debonair young man had fled from Paris.
He had been found by Police in a chalet in the
Alps near Chamonix. It was reported that he
was found suffering from a gun wound which
ultimately killed him. The official verdict was sui-
cide. But many ordinary people had lost money
from his activities and the French public with its
penchant for the refrain "Nous sommes trahis"
wanted a scapegoat. Various shady right-wing or-

ganisations claimed that the government had arranged for the police intentionally to kill Stavisky in order to protect influential politicians. It was Dreyfus all over again and the political crisis that followed grumbled on and on just at the time that Hitler was consolidating his position across the Rhine.

Antisemitism, never far from the surface in French society, became the rage all over again and riots and demonstrations continued during the Popular Front government of Leon Blum, himself a Jew. It was this government that was holding office when Vahan and Nerissa arrived. The Stavisky affair left France internally weakened and divided, and it was during this period that Vahan heard the phrase "Better Hitler than Blum" even from people whom they had invited to dinner. There was this great difference between French anti-Semitism and German. Nazi antisemitism was the irrational and ugly passion of the gutter come to power. It was primarily fuelled by the lower middle classes and by the dispossessed of the streets. French anti-Semitism, on the other hand, was most active in the elite and the upper middle classes. It was undisputedly not a working class movement. Of course there were many exceptions on both sides in both countries, but Vahan was surprised to find how many of the respectable Catholic professionals who came to their table issued doom-laden warnings about the influx of Jewish refugees, and for whom in the end and against all the evidence – *Dreyfus etait coupable*.

These people knew perfectly well that the As-adourians were Armenian. Like so many of the French elite, they were well aware of the massa-cres and deportations suffered by the Armenians during the Great War. Furthermore, almost with-out exception they were highly sympathetic, and openly expressed that sympathy. But for them, there seemed to be no comparison at all between the Armenian experience in 1915 and the purely verbal antisemitism which these respectable Cath-olic bourgeoisie brazenly acknowledged and par-ticipated in. After all, the last time there had been any major deportation of the Jews in the modern world was the expulsion from Spain, now almost three hundred years ago. Most of these guests at Nerissa's dinner table of course never contem-plated any parallels, as they repeated their preju-dices and their racist jokes.

Nerissa's French was as impeccable and ac-cent-free as her English and so conversation was easy and genial. Being an Avakian, Nerissa could never restrain herself in these discussions, even when she was the hostess. However, the fact that her son was Jewish – a fact always acknowledged – seemed perversely to lessen the force of her ar-guments. French high society, however deeply prejudiced, was always polite and, whenever she entered the fray, argument would cease – much to her disappointment.

Meanwhile back in Istanbul, the merchant house of Asadourian et fils became more and more prominent in the commercial life of the city. Unlike Karekin, who all his life concentrated entirely on Lancashire textiles, Garabed was sensitive to the declining competitiveness of Lancashire. He decided to import Egyptian cotton to feed the growing Turkish textile industry. So, after Ara was married to a young Armenian girl – yet another orphan from the thousands left abandoned in Anatolia – Garabed sent him to Cairo to open a branch office there,

For the next three years, each summer Vahan and Nerissa would take the Simplon-Orient train to join their families in Istanbul. Harry, Olga and family would also come from London. Vahan would attend every day at the office with Garabed and Ara, whose wife and two daughters would also arrive from Egypt. Garabed would hire a large country house set in the midst of gardens with vines and fruit trees, in a far-out suburb of the city on the Asian side – Suadiye – to accommodate them all. The village was then in the deep countryside, but it was one of the last stops of the ferry service, running from Uskudar along the Asian coastline. The men would go to work at the office in Pera, changing ferries in Uskudar, and would return in the afternoons. By the summer of 1939, for various reasons, including a school exam that Hakim was due to sit, Nerissa had decided not to make the trip that year. Instead the plan was to meet Olga and her British family in the station in Paris on their own way to Istanbul for the summer. Vahan would make a purely business trip later, in October.

Chapter 9

Munich

In the late-thirties pacifism ran deep in both French and British society. The trauma and horrors of the Great War had not been forgotten, nor should they have been. "All that was best in British society" supported Chamberlain when he returned from Munich waving his pathetic piece of paper. Harry and his father William, were no exception despite the fact that they were military men. In due course, particularly after the unopposed march by Hitler into Prague despite all his assurances, many would claim that they were always sceptical about the events in Munich – but in most cases that was simply untrue. The public supported their Prime Minister's efforts. It was not cowardice, nor moral decadence – it was perfectly reasonable and logical to be desperately keen to avoid a war which, with the growing element of air-power, the effects of which were exaggerated even by the airmen themselves, was going to be devastating for everyone.

Conrad was fifteen at the time of Munich. Olga had imposed the Avakian style of debate in her own marriage and Conrad and his two younger siblings had always been encouraged to put forward their views in the long discussions which went on over the dinner table. There would have been a time when Colonel William might have muttered something about children being seen but not heard, but he had mellowed, influenced by the Avakians during his stay in Constantinople and his son's marriage. So, when present, he no longer huffed and puffed at either childish or feminine arguments.

Of course neither little Billy, only six at the time of Munich, nor Natalie, had any real idea of what was at stake at Munich and kept quiet as the family pondered together. But Olga had strong views and intuitively hated the way in which the Czechs, without any consultation, had been shamefully abandoned to a regime she considered barbarous. She never liked the strutting German military, SS or SA. German was the one language that the Bolsetsi elite had not comfortably embraced. However she did not need to understand what the man on the newsreels was actually saying to take a dislike to him and to form her opinions accordingly.

Conrad was calmer and in fairness, even at the age of fifteen more understanding and frankly better educated than his mother. Although his instinct was to agree with her, he listened hard to his father as they discussed the matter the day after watching Chamberlain's return from his meeting with Hitler on the newsreels in the local cinema.

"Olga, my dear," Harry said, as they were all seated at the dinner table, "Don't get excited. Consider what you are saying – what it boils down to is that you would like us to go to war – war! –

with Germany."

"No, oh no – I don't want that. I just want us to be firm and to stand up to that horrid little man."

"But my soul – horrid though he might be, he happens to be the current leader of the German nation. All he appears to be requiring is that those Germans currently living in the edges of Czechoslovakia should come back into Germany – something which they themselves appear to want passionately."

"Er, father – surely those Sudeten Germans have never been part of any German state, so why say 'come back'."

"Well yes, you are right son, but that issue is only a debating point. We live in an era of nationalism, and the fanatic disciples of the nation-state require everyone within the state to be homogeneous, and let's face it the Czech state...."

"But Harry", interrupted Olga, "the French had a solemn treaty and we too had obligations. Just to abandon a people who have consistently been such a support to the Western democracies and to France in particular, is so...."

"War! Both of you stop and think. What you are both demanding is that in order to prevent German Sudetenland hiving itself off from the somewhat artificial state created at Versailles and joining Germany, you are prepared to go to war. You are prepared to send young men to die in their thousands. You want the bombers to fly over and drop bombs on enemy cities and kill more thousands, women and children included. You want the inevitable concomitant consequence of starvation and disease to strike. And for what? So that a couple of million Germans living in a fairly closely defined area should not be allowed to become part of Germany?"

"Father – of course war is terrible. You know that better than most having seen a lot of it at first-hand. But isn't it arguable that there might be occasions when not standing up and going to war is a worse alternative. You may have persuaded me that on this occasion it might not be the right moment, but Dad, I'm not so sure that Mum isn't right and that we should stand and fight if necessary."

"Oh God, Conrad, no, God no, surely I am not advocating a war am I?" called out Olga. "I just feel…"

"God has got nothing to do with it, Mum."

"Don't be prissy and pompous. You're just parroting your grandfather Karekin. Ah, Billy, you've been very quiet – trying not to be noticed. Come on, bedtime for you my lad. Natalie, see that the men help you clear up. Say goodnight Billy."

Poor Natalie – neither Conrad nor Harry made the slightest effort to help her as she cleared up, instead continuing their discussion ranging around issues such as 'balance of power'; traditional theories of opposing any one dominant power in Europe; sanctity of treaties; and pure national interest.

Ironically, exactly the same discussion was going on in the Asadourian family in Paris – with almost exactly the same differences. Nerissa was repeating her sister Olga's arguments, though having a smattering of German she knew what Hitler was screaming in the newsreels. In her own inimitable style, she was arguing from logic and careful analysis, unlike Olga who as always tended to argue straight from the heart. Meanwhile, Vahan was parroting his brother-in-law in London and warning Nerissa about the logical consequences of demanding that France acknowledge its obligations to Czechoslvakia and stand up to the bully in the centre of Europe.

In this respect, the two families' reactions were extraordinarily similar. This was not however true of the leaders of the two democracies. Having virtually handed over a democratic country, with perfectly defensible borders and a modern army, to a rapacious bullying Germany, Chamberlain remained sure of his own righteousness – that self-rightcousness backed up by a Christian rectitude that was such an unattractive part of his character. The contrast with Daladier who had been his co-negotiator at Munich acting for France, was striking. As Daladier flew back and his plane circled preparing to land at Le Bourget, he saw down below crowds awaiting his arrival. He commented to his staff – "They are going to tear me limb from limb." He, at least, was fully aware that his abandonment of a country with whom France had a clear and binding treaty of alliance, a country which had supported France through thick and thin, was a shameful act of dis-honour. But it was more than that – it was a sure and absolute sign that France could no longer op-erate as an independent great power.

In the last resort the whole French delegation at Munich was forced to accept the fact that they could never again stand up to Germany on their own. They either had to recreate the Russian alli-ance of the Great War era – anathema to the pas-sionately anti-communist conservative politicians running French foreign policy – or they would have to make sure that Britain was on board. So, when Chamberlain insisted on appeasement and on giving in to Hitler, they simply had to tag along.

A few months later, in March 1939 Hitler sim-ply marched into the now defenceless Prague and took over what was left of Czechoslovakia. By then, both Harry and William Bridgeman in England and Vahan in France had changed their minds, as had so many others.

Munich was from the start and has always re-mained controversial. It is nearly always a mis-take to try and appease a bully, neither the one in the school playground, nor the nation-state in the cut-throat community of nation-states. But there is a problem – how to identify who exactly is the bully?

With the comfort of hindsight, it is always easy to denigrate decisions taken by honourable men at the time. It does not necessarily follow that those who want to find sharp and clear-cut solutions to complicated political problems are always right, or that those who are inclined to look for peaceful compromise are always wrong. Harry and Vahan could have added, in talking to their families, that consideration should be given as to how many possible wars may have been averted by patient diplomacy and goodwill – and as to how many wars may have been caused by firebrands not prepared to seek a compromise.

Nevertheless!

Could it not be said, at least, that in the long run it is usually best for any nation to act honourably in any situation. But even relying on 'honour' is a dangerous concept. National honour can be a suspect motivation – there is so often an element of male arrogance in the conception. Having contemplated all this, turned it over and over in his mind and discussed it all with both Olga and Conrad, Harry came to a clear and final conclusion by the beginning of the summer. He decided that for the French government to have abandoned her ally Czechoslovakia to her fate, was a major moral lapse, and more to the point was in the end fatal for France itself. It did not cross Harry's mind that his own government was also at fault by being highly instrumental in driving France into that fatal decision.

Chapter 10

The summer of 1939 begins

In March 1939 Hitler simply walked into Prague and took over the whole of the rest of Czechoslovakia. Chamberlain now swung right round and began shooting off 'guarantees' all over Eastern Europe – in particular to Poland. Hitler assumed that this was face-saving posturing and in a sense this view was completely justified. He could see that Chamberlain had not been prepared to stand up for Czechoslovakia. That was a situation where he could have had firm Russian support, where there was a well-armed modern Czech army entrenched behind a strong mountain barrier, and where the continued existence of this last bastion of democratic government in Eastern Europe was an obvious British interest. If he did not act there, why should he go to war on an issue – Danzig – which was of no concern to Britain, where there would be no Soviet support, and where any intervention would be on behalf of an autocratic regime as dictatorial as that of Germany.

So Hitler began his preparations for a war with another Slav country, a war which he felt he had been cheated out of at Munich. Great Britain did indeed begin rearming very soon after Munich – a rearmament programme that accelerated after Hitler's march into Prague. However, it is manifestly untrue that the time gained by the capitulation of Munich increased British preparedness for war. Statistically, the German increase in their own re-arming programme far outweighed the Anglo-French response.

The march into Prague and the incorporation of the whole of Bohemia and Moravia into the German Reich abruptly ended all the arguments that had raged about Munich. Both the Bridgemans came right round to support the feeling that war was now inevitable and that Nazi Germany had to be stopped. Ironically, Olga now began to have second thoughts. She had listened to all Harry's arguments about the horrors of a coming war, and was now afraid for her family, just as all the men in her family were all for standing up and being counted. She wrote to her sister Sima in Italy telling her of the change of mood in London. 'I awake in the mornings', she wrote, 'and see that the children get off to school and Harry to work – then I begin to feel afraid as I think of the bombs and gas and death in the streets. Then in the afternoon, when young Billy comes dashing in from school, all male-cub energy and bursting with news, I become brave and British again. But the fears start all over again the next day'.

It had become clear to most people in Britain that war was now coming – clear to the British public, though, ironically, not clear to Hitler or the German High Command. This is not to say that had he been aware of this change of attitude he would not have invaded Poland. Nevertheless he was not, and genuinely believed that neither of the Western allies would in the end lift a finger to help Poland.

The issue for the Bridgeman family as April turned to May was whether the usual family trip to Istanbul was going to take place this summer or not. Olga, despite her fears, did not want to change their routine or return the tickets already booked. They were due to leave the very day after the schools closed for the summer, which this year was on the 15th July. They were booked to return on the 15th September a few days before the schools reopened. Harry himself could not be away so long from his work at the Admiralty and arranged to come out himself on his own in the middle of August.

So it was that once again two first-class cabins were taken up on the carriage leaving Victoria station for Paris to join the Simplon-Orient express for Istanbul. Olga and Natalie were in one room and Conrad and Billy were in the compartment next door with a small communicating bathroom in between.

As Vahan and Nerissa had decided not to go to Istanbul this summer, it was agreed that they would meet Olga and her British family at the Gare du Nord and sit with them in their carriage as it trundled its way round the 'ceinture' to join the Simplon-Orient express at the Gare de Lyon. This duly occurred and they welcomed

Olga and the children when the Golden Arrow pulled into Paris. Squaring the brown-uniformed attendant with a suitable sweetener, they clambered into the coach and stayed on it as it began its cumbersome journey round to the Gare de Lyon. Nerissa and Olga quickly completed all their sisterly hugs and kisses which were so much part of the Avakian routine. Before they could go too far with their nostalgic reminiscences, Nerissa, who did not care for idle chit-chat, launched into what was at the back of the mind of all the adults.

"Olga, my soul, what is the current feeling in London? Are we going to have a war? What does Harry think?"

"Well, to be honest I can't really say what Harry believes. He had been in favour of the agreement that Chamberlain brought back from Munich, but now he has adopted a determination to stand up to Germany regardless of the consequences, which is very English if you know what I mean. On the other hand, I am not so sure anymore. Why should we send our young men to die for a militaristic Poland that...."

"Oh mother," interrupted Conrad who had been listening eagerly, "it wouldn't matter if it was Timbuctoo he was threatening – we have to put a stop to it now and that is what Dad believes."

Nerissa was an Avakian and was quite used to 15 or 16-year olds interrupting and putting their point of view – something that had always been encouraged by Karekin. She then said –

73

"I agree Conrad my love – but listen is there anything, after all, that we can actually do practically to help the Poles. Surely we can only be of any real use to them if we can get Soviet Russia on our side."

"The problem with that", said Vahan joining in for the first time, "is that we have here in France a government that is bitterly anti-communist and not keen to open any negotiations with Moscow."

"But I thought you had a left-wing government – the Radicals aren't they."

"My dear Olga – in Britain you have Conservative governments which are often fairly left-wing – but here in France we have ostensibly left-wing governments which are always very right-wing. But at least we have a strong army – led by an officer corps which is Catholic and reactionary, but which is I believe efficient. We have an unassailable defence in the Maginot line and the Germans will have to fight through a defended Belgium if they are to get at us."

"But Uncle Vahan – how are we to help the Poles if all we are going to do is sit behind your Maginot line and defend Belgium."

There was a short silence.

"It is a question, my boy, of winning the war 'eventually'. The German flood will break on our defences, and then the British Naval blockade will eat away at them as it did in 1914 – and in the end peace will arrive and Germany will have to evacuate Poland."

"But are we going to have a war in the next few

months?" said Nerissa.

There was again a short silence. Then Conrad lightened the mood by grinning and saying –

"No way, Auntie, no way, not until we have enjoyed our holiday and got back home."

The discussions ranged on – and messages for the family in Bolis passed on, until eventually the coach arrived and was added on to the front of the Simplon-Orient express waiting at the Gare de Lyon. Then it was time for Vahan, Nerissa and Hakim to leave. There had been an atmosphere of gloom that had pervaded the talk of war throughout the afternoon, as the train had shunted back and forth around Paris. That gloom resulted in an outpouring of emotion when it came to the moment of departure. Nerissa's fierce embrace of her sister stretched into eternity. Vahan, holding Hakim's hand, with Nerissa alongside, stood waving in a surprisingly empty platform as the train slowly steamed out on its journey to the east.

Chapter 11

Billy recalls his last journey out

Memories of the past are sometimes like flashes of lightening that illuminates one place or one moment in time so vividly that one can recall every little detail of the event being recalled. Then everything before and after fades, leaving only a disembodied imprint in sharp focus.

Recalling an event from the past creates a whole new life, even several lives. We all live many of our past moments and experiences as a narrative that we have fashioned in our minds. Sometimes we are creating that artificial narrative in our memory even before we have completed the actual experience. Memories are constructed and re-thought over and over again, almost from the very first moment.

"Life is not what one has actually lived but what one supposedly remembers and the manner in which one remembers it in order to recount it to others."

This was what Billy remembered, or thought he remembered, from that last trip out to his grandparents in the summer of 1939.

"I was bursting with excitement as usual when we arrived at Victoria station and headed for the platform on which the Golden Arrow was waiting. My Dad had come to see us off. As always we had an enormous number of trunks and cases. Presents for the family in Istanbul were enough to fill one whole case on their own. Then there were Mama's hats and dresses, clothes for Dad when he arrived and a case each for me, Conrad and Natalie. All this luggage was loaded onto a couple of the stand-up trolleys. Father had got hold of two porters and I saw them ahead of us pushing the whole lot down the platform past the waiting train to the dark blue sleeping car which was always at the far end of the train. When we caught them up, they had stopped by the words "Paris – Milan – Belgrade – Sofia – Istanbul" on a white plaque on the side of the coach.

As well as the large cases, we each had our own travelling bag. Mine contained my pyjamas, spare pants and socks for three nights and some toys and books carefully picked out for me by Conrad. Conrad was carrying his own bag and also carrying mine, so I couldn't hold his hand. I certainly wasn't going to hold Natalie's so I was trotting along next to Daddy holding onto his jacket.

Standing at the door at the end of the coach was the usual attendant dressed in a brown uniform. He had a list attached to a heavy pad and ticked off our names as mother handed him our tickets. I saw my father chatting to him as the porters handed up all the cases. He slipped a note, obviously money, into the attendant's hand. I saw it was white and crinkly so it must have been £5. I wondered what it was for, but by then I had scrambled up the iron steps which were surprisingly high – or so they seemed to be to me then.

I can never quite recall the actual departure. I know that there must have been long and lingering kisses between my Mum and Dad, but I just do not remember them. I do recall that it was always a ritual that Conrad and I would get out onto the platform again after we had left our bags on the beds in our berth. We strolled up with Daddy to inspect the steam engine which was to take us as far as Paris. I was just 7 years-old but understood that this engine would not take us further than Paris. In Paris our coach would be attached to another train which would take us the rest of the way to where my other grandfather and grandmother lived. After inspecting the engine carefully, we would walk back and Conrad would lift me up onto the train after I kissed Father goodbye. It is odd that I do not actually recall the kisses and the hugs. Even at that age I was aware that as a family we were different to my school-friends. They shook hands with their fathers – even sometimes with their mothers. We always hugged and kissed. Just occasionally – not wanting to be different, I would be a bit embarrassed at the school gates, and this would make my mother smile and nod her head instead. But my father never stood for it and would always give me a hug or a kiss. But whereas I can remember vividly my mother's embraces, I can't recall those of my Dad.

I was aware that I had two quite different families as I grew up. My father and his father, my grandfather, were both military men and there was an air of a military background in our home in Purley. I had an enormous collection of tin soldiers – whole cavalry regiments – cannon – musketeers – axemen – archers – all mixed up with no regard to the different eras from which they came. I moved them up and down the great Turkish carpet in the dining room, which was the official battleground. It was always empty during the day and I didn't have to clear up if there was no formal dinner arranged for the evening.

Beautifully painted, glowing with bright colours, I never got round to the tedious task of doing the painting myself. It was always Conrad who would carefully and painstakingly colour each one when I was given another box of grey tin soldiers and present them to me with a grin at my wondering pleasure. Sometimes even Natalie would help him on a rainy day. I don't think I ever bothered to thank him, other than with a quick kiss on his cheek, as I hurried off to add them to my army. Somehow it was a natural part of my life – that was what older brothers were for.

But I had a second family – my mother's family some of whom seemed to live all over the world but whose roots were with my other grandfather and grandmother who lived in Istanbul. From a very early age, we would all go to visit them every summer. This year was already my fourth trip on this train journey.

As usual, once the train left – it was I believe almost always at 10 o'clock at night – I would already be in my pyjamas and lying on the top bunk, sure that I wouldn't be able to sleep. However the gentle shaking of the coach as the train trundled through the night would send me to sleep almost immediately. Conrad's light was always on above his lower bunk as he lay and read, but it did not bother me at all. The train reached the docks at Dover but I would still be fast asleep. Conrad would time it very carefully and shake me gently as the manoeuvring of the train onto the ferry began. Not bothering with the little ladder he lifted me down as I slowly awoke. Then we would lie together on his bunk with our heads against the window looking out at all the activity outside. Conrad would have already lifted the green blinds halfway up so we could see everything. This was now the third time that I had been able to be up and watch how the train got onto the ferry. I had seen it all before and soon sleep overcame me again. I never remembered when Conrad lifted me back up onto my bunk, but that was certainly where I was when I woke up the next morning.

Conrad was gently shaking me and told me that we were a bit late and that Mum and Natalie had already gone to breakfast.

"Come along Billy – hurry up, go and have a pee and splash your face. See I have all your clothes laid out. Get on with it."

I flung myself down off the bed into his arms and ran into the little bathroom. When I got back he helped me with my grey shirt and shorts. He tied my tie for me as I fumbled with the buttons on my pants. We then walked quickly down the corridor to the Restaurant car. Neither I nor Conrad wanted to miss breakfast. I just loved that breakfast on the train – bacon and eggs, perfect toast and wonder of wonders, a half grapefruit already cut up so I didn't get messy.

As Dad was not with us, we all stayed in the coach when it moved out of the Gare du Nord to make the long journey to the other station, going backwards and forwards and taking hours and hours – or so it seemed to me. What was different on this occasion was that Aunty Nerissa, my mother's sister, and her husband Uncle Vahan were at the Gare du Nord with their own little boy Hakim when we arrived. Hakim was a year older than me and he had the dark looks of Conrad. I vaguely knew that there was something different about him, but not exactly what it was. They all came into our coach, and I saw Uncle Vahan handing some money to our attendant, who never ever seemed to sleep. I can remember that even if at night if I ever peeped out of our compartment door, he was always seated there at the far end of the corridor and would give me a sharp look so I would scuttle back inside at once.

My Aunt, Uncle and cousin stayed with us the whole time as the coach clanked its way laboriously in and out of stations until we finally arrived at the Gare de Lyon. We were all sitting in Mum's and Natalie's compartment and it was a bit of a squeeze.

As we travelled round, what I now know was

called the 'ceinture', the grown-ups entered into a long conversation about the coming war, which meant nothing much to me of course and I began to fidget. My father hated me fidgeting so I was usually good at controlling it – but he wasn't here. Also Conrad was sitting with his arm round Hakim and had been very assiduous in putting him at his ease. I can remember, with a sense of guilt, that I felt jealous – his arm should have been round me, but I had to sit on the floor. He was intensely interested in the adult talk and had no time to see to me. Mama, seeing me fidgeting, got out a pack of cards and told me to go next door to our compartment and take Hakim with me. Hakim could only speak French, whilst I could only speak English and I felt it would be a disaster. But nevertheless once we were away from Conrad I felt better, and we got round to playing Snap – the beds were of course all folded away so we had plenty of room.

At last the carriage arrived and got attached to the Simplon-Orient Express waiting at the platform. Somehow, the parting at the Gare de Lyon was very emotional that year – even at seven I was aware of it – the talk that the adults had indulged in had seemed to make them all tearful. We hugged and kissed for what seemed like an age and waved madly at the little group left on the platform as the train slowly steamed off to make its way through the Alps.

"Birra, Panini, Arangiata!"

I have passed through and even stopped at

the station of Domodossola many times in my life both before and after the war. Yet despite all those memorable occasions I have never seen the town itself. I wonder what it is like?

At Milan station, waiting on the platform, as the train steamed into the huge glass hall, were my mother's older sister Aunty Sima and her husband – Uncle Nicolai. I was leaning out of the window – 'e pericoloso sporgersi' – held firmly round my waist by Conrad and I was the first to see them, alarming Conrad by waving at them frantically. I saw at once that they were carrying a huge wooden box of Italian peaches. Why do I remember those peaches as being so particularly tasty?

They came up on board. The train usually stood for over an hour in Milan station. They brought up those wonderful peaches and a great blue tin of caviar. The peaches were handed to Natalie and she and I and Conrad sat in our compartment stuffing ourselves with the peaches, until the juices were running down and dropping from our chins. Both doors to the washroom between the two compartments were left open and we could see across the shower that the three adults were passing the blue tin round and dipping into the black gooey mess with a teaspoon each. Uncle Nicolai had also brought with him a bottle of colourless liquid which just looked like water – and this bottle was also being passed round and the 'water' drunk from the train toothmugs. I recall Mum and Aunty Sima hugging and kissing each other and giggling together, as they sipped away at what I thought at the time was water. It must have been vodka I suppose. In any event, it was all a good deal more cheerful than the family meeting in Paris. It was only later that I came to know that Aunty Nerissa had always been more serious than the other sisters and had never really liked chit-chat.

Once again, whereas I can recall vividly every detail of that hour we spent stationery in Milan, I cannot remember the goodbyes or the hugs and kisses that must have accompanied our departure.

The next day when I awoke we were already in Yugoslavia. The train was going much slower. I was awake before Conrad for once. I slipped down off the bunk and got dressed on my own and without any help – though I did not bother to put on my tie. I went out into the corridor and knocked at my mother's door. There was a whispered 'Come in'. Only Natalie was there and she was already fully dressed. She said that mother had already gone to breakfast, that she herself was going right now and that I was to wake Conrad and follow. She went out and I did as I was told though I first watched her walk down the corridor, nod at the attendant sitting on his stool, and go on.

This was usually the moment, once the attendant had seen that the occupants of a room had gone to breakfast, that he would come to make up the beds and stow them away, leaving only the seat for the rest of the day. But on this occasion he did not, but stood waiting at the end of the corridor. I ran into our room, woke up Conrad and said that I would go on after Natalie and join them. He nodded and got up to wash himself in the bathroom.

I went out and along the corridor. To my surprise I found that the door to the next coach was locked. So that was why the attendant had been waiting. He came behind me and opened the door with a key. I went across the swaying couplings and into the next coach. But instead of another quiet corridor I found myself in a coach with wooden seats on either side of a central passage – all filled with people, animals, children, rough looking men and all talking at the top of their voices. The whole coach – or so it seemed to me at the time – turned and stared at me, and the coach went quiet. I turned round and ran back and hammered on the door. The brown-coated attendant was still there and opened the door at once with a great grin on his face. I scampered back to Conrad. I was frightened, but knew that I ought not to be, so I said nothing to Conrad as he finished dressing.

He gave me a questioning look. Without actually lying I explained that I had come back to keep him company. Once he was ready we duly passed through several coaches of these people all wrapped up in heavily layered clothes, though it was very warm weather outside. I held on tight to Conrad's hand as we passed through, skirting

85

shabby suitcases, wrapped bundles of clothes or rugs and even animals in wicker cages.

Later that morning when we were all back, the attendant called on mother and advised her that we should not drink from the tap as the water going to the cabins was not drinkable anymore and was for washing only. The weather had been getting hotter and hotter. He said that there would be bottled water available which he would bring on board at the next major stop. The fact that we couldn't drink the water seemed to make me more thirsty and I think we all felt it. As always I complained to Conrad who just smiled. Then the train began to slow down.

I was kneeling on the seat looking out, my nose and bare knees pressed against the window, and I could feel the sweat trickling down my neck. The great train began to slow down in order to come to an unscheduled halt alongside a low platform somewhere in the middle of the Balkans.

The train juddered to a stop. Clouds of steam arose from below the carriage, mixing with the smoke belching from the engine in front, and this obscured my view for a moment. When this cleared, I saw the sleepy station, bathed in the bright yellow of the hot midday sunshine, dusty and quiet. On the platform I could see only one lonely figure – the stationmaster – dressed in a dark blue uniform, with a red-braided officers cap, a whistle hanging round his neck, and a little green flag in his right hand.

Conrad, who was also in the compartment

laughed out loud, grabbed the glass ewer that usually held drinking water, but which was now empty and ran out into the corridor.

Hordes of young men, or so it seemed to me, jumped down from the carriages – both from the large blue international sleeping cars and from the green wooden-seated local wagons. Laughing and eager, jostling each other, good-humoured but nevertheless competitive, they all made a dash for the solitary water tap, which could be seen on the wall of the tiny airless ticket office. All had bottles or cups of one kind or another in their hands.

They overwhelmed the stationmaster as they ran past him, yelling incomprehensible words at each other. I saw Conrad in the middle of them all, with the wagon-lits glass flask in his hands, eagerly pressing on towards that single dripping tap. I lost sight of the tap as the crowd gathered round it, but I soon saw young men pushing their way back through the crowd, carrying their cups and bottles carefully so as not to spill the precious cold water. They all walked back to the train, which stood hissing and steaming and making loud rumbling noises alongside the low inadequate platform. The very size of the train dwarfed and somehow diminished the low buildings of the little station, and the crumbling village houses clustered around.

The length of the train was such that it stretched beyond the platform of the little station and across the level crossing at the forward end.

Here, a dusty unpaved road crossed the railway line. Waiting patiently to cross over to the other side was a line of carts, with silent grizzled men sitting hunched up on the front, holding the reins of tired and scraggy-looking horses, mules and donkeys. In the back of the carts there were sacks and seated alongside them children, equally quiet with large staring eyes, and women clothed in bright colourful skirts with scarves around their heads.

Old Europe sat still, staring patiently at the bright young men eagerly filling their bottles at the station tap, and said nothing. They waited for the iron monster to move on and enable them to get on with their lives.

The train hooted. The stationmaster began blowing his whistle frantically, waving his flag and shouting at the young men. The train gave a sudden jerk, almost hurling me off my perch. All the young men, still laughing and shouting, began running back to the train and jumping on, as very slowly it began to move, gliding past the platform amidst smoke and steam.

I strained and strained but could not see Conrad anywhere, as the train slowly began to gather speed. A sudden passing fear gripped hold of me – I can recall the terror to this day. The train clattered across the level crossing. Through the tears of fear beginning to flow into my eyes, I saw a young boy at the front of the first cart, sitting next to a weather-beaten old man. The boy was staring at me as the train passed. I raised my hand against the window in a gentle wave and tried to smile at him, but the village boy simply stared back at me, without moving a muscle, as the train went by.

I recall falling back onto the seat and then bursting into silent sobs as the train picked up speed, and bustled away. What was I thinking? After all these years I don't know anymore. When he came in, Conrad never asked me what I was crying about; he simply put down the flask of water, sat down beside me, put his arms round my shoulders and pressed my face into his chest.

That particular incident in which nothing at all really happened remains as a vivid spark lighting up the past, but then everything fades away again. Later that day as the train went on through mountains and over viaducts, I recall running down the corridor with terrified screams of delight at being chased by Conrad who was pretending to be a train chasing after me with fists pounding one after the other. Without thinking I opened what I thought was our door to escape and burst in on a middle-aged couple who were sort of entwined and who stared up at me from their seat. I ran straight out past Conrad who had come running up. He apologised profusely in French. Conrad was always wonderful with languages, speaking Italian fluently as well as French and even a little Armenian.

Finally – finally – after what seemed to me to be a whole week – I recall the arrival at Sirkedji station; all the excitement of people embracing, laughing and crying, a blur of familiar faces all of whom I recognised from our trip the year before. I was picked up – put down – smothered into skirts smelling faintly of moth-balls. It was the beginning of a memorable summer."

Chapter 12

Istanbul

Billy had been named after his grandfather – William Bridgeman. He had fair hair and bluish-green eyes. He was tall and wiry for his age. His Avakian blood came out in the huge brown eyes looking on rather incredulously at life with a sort of naïve wonder.

Once the welcomes on Platform 1 of Sirkedji station had finally subsided, some of those who had come to the station to welcome the British contingent crossed over to Platform 3 to board the local train running back down the same line to Makrikoy, the suburb where the family lived. But the luggage and most of the family went out through the chandeliered main entrance and into a fleet of cars waiting outside. The Avakians were still in the same house up the road from the Cobancesme station, up the hill past the Vali Effendi racecourse. The area had not changed very much since the end of the Great War and the fields stretched out on either side, once the few houses straggling up from the station were passed.

The house was set right on the road up from Makrikoy. It had a very large garden sweeping back to orchards and woods at the far end. The grounds were surrounded by a high wall, with one door further on beyond the front door also leading out onto the street. The main door itself opened straight into a large hall where almost all the family activities took place. The stairs to the upper floors swept down into the centre of this room. On one side of the stairs was a large dining table and chairs, with a door beyond leading to the kitchens. On the other side of the stairs was a door leading to the formal sitting room, and another door to Karekin's study. Dotted about the whole room were settees and comfortable but rather shabby sofas, resting on the marble floor, covered with exquisite, if now somewhat faded, Persian carpets.

The house was large but nevertheless Conrad and Billy had to share a room. Seta, the youngest of the sisters, was still unmarried and living at home. Then there was Haik, Karekin's adopted son. Natalie slept with Olga until Harry's arrival. From the start Karekin shamelessly spoilt little Billy. Despite having four daughters he only had Olga's children as biological grandchildren. Liberal though he was where girls were concerned, nevertheless it was the boy on whom he lavished attention. For some reason, unclear to Billy or Conrad, his warmth was unquestionably centred on Billy to the exclusion of both Conrad, and his own adopted son yegrort Haik. Of course he hid it fairly well. The admirable Armineh, his wife, would never have actually 'spoilt' any child, but she made quite sure that Natalie who was at a very awkward age, never felt left out.

Haik was a year older than Conrad who had

just reached 16. However he looked and acted much younger. He was still going to the boys section of the American Robert College, though the school was of course closed for the long summer holiday. He had few friends and from the start clung on to the cheerful and tolerant Conrad, more than just hero-worshipping him. The two youths would go out together taking the train into town. They would occasionally pop into a café to drink tea in those delicate Bolsetsi glass cups. They would take trips on the ferries going up the Bosphorus or across to the Asian side.

Olga never allowed Billy to join them on these excursions and, once again, Billy began to feel sharp pangs of jealousy as he had in previous years. For the first time he recognised the feelings as just that – jealousy. After all, it was impossible actually to dislike the gentle Haik, but he found it was very difficult to control his emotions. In the garden, Conrad would set up a badminton court and Billy would make up a foursome with Natalie. But if Aunty Seta wandered down and joined them, Billy would be dropped and he would have to sit on the grass and watch.

Seta was still a bubbling irrepressible girl, congenitally unable to keep still. She was not a grand beauty like her sister Olga, but she looked and acted much younger than her age and the boys could not help but think of her as if she was in her early twenties. She was sporty and was open and very natural with both her nephew Conrad, and her adopted brother Haik. Both boys had passed puberty and both harboured sexual fantasies about the lively Seta, who had no idea about the effect that she had on the two boys as she bounced about the badminton court.

Language was never a barrier in the Istanbul of the late thirties. Although now far less cosmopolitan than when it was Constantinople, the capital of the Ottoman Empire, nevertheless most Bolsetsi could still move effortlessly from one language to another whenever the occasion demanded it. In any case, for Conrad and Haik there was no problem as Haik's English, albeit fairly Americanised, had become impeccable. So it was, that lying together on the bed in Haik's room, staring up at the ceiling, they were able to chat together easily one afternoon about ten days after the Bridgemans had arrived.

"Haik, I'm curious, I know that you are adopted – tell me do you know how you came to end up in our family."

"I don't really know much. I believe I was plucked out of my mother's arms as she lay dying. We were in Smyrna on the quayside as the whole town burned behind us, set alight by the Turkish army. It was a terrible catastrophe, I believe, but it is not talked about very much anymore as the Turks don't like to remember it."

"Yes – but listen, who picked you up from your Mum's arms and what happened."

"I am not sure – I was never actually told, but I think it was Haik who was mother and father's son. They have never said so directly, and Marie just shakes her head whenever I ask for more details. Anyway that is what I have worked out for myself. That is why my name is Haik, and why sometimes people call me 'yegrort' Haik."

"What happened to him?"

"He died in the fire – of that I am certain."

"But how then did you get away?"

"Well I believe that he put me into the hands of a British sailor on a boat that had come alongside, before dying himself. Father adopted me when I got to Constantinople in the British battleship."

There was a short silence as both boys lay back. Conrad contemplated the story that Haik was telling him and could not make sense of it – there were so many inconsistencies. He thought to himself how much more persistent he himself would have been to find out more, if it had been his story.

"What is it like to be adopted?"

"Oh Conrad, I don't know how to answer that one. After all I have never known what it is like to have natural biological parents. This is all I have ever known, so it seems just like every other parent-child relationship."

"Seta is your sister then."

"Well, yes – adopted."

"She is thirteen or so years older than you isn't she – I mean she is very – er – attractive isn't she."

"Well yes I suppose so – what are you getting at Conrad?"

"Oh I don't know. I find her very... er... you know lovely to look at. She is such a good sport and ..."

At this point Conrad's vocabulary gave out. He had been having sexual fantasies about his young Aunt ever since he had arrived and was wondering whether his cousin had the same. On the other hand he was slightly ashamed.

There was a short silence as both boys contemplated the charms of the sister/Aunt. Then somewhat huskily Haik said –

"Conrad – do you love her then?"

"For heavens sake Haik, of course not. I don't know anything about love. I mean I love my family of course – but.. er.. the other kind... I mean I don't think I have ever fallen in love with a girl. I did kiss a girl once – or rather she kissed me if I am to be truly honest. But love – no. As for Seta I just think of her body sometimes that's all."

"Well I've never kissed or been kissed by anyone – I mean ... er ... sexily. But love – that is something I do understand. I love you Conrad."

Conrad remained completely silent – though the silence was no longer quite as companionable as before. Without making any great issue of it, he rolled off the bed and stood up looking down at Haik who had blushed red, but just managed to find the moral strength to look back at him steadily.

"Please don't be angry with me Conrad – I'm only telling the truth. It is not something I have ever said to anyone before. Please don't..."

Tears welled up in Haik's eyes and he turned his face away so as not to look into Conrad's rather stern eyes. But Conrad saw the tears, and his own heart melted as it always did at other people's distress. There was no way that he would leave the boy in that state of mortified embarrassment. So before leaving he bent down and gave him a long lingering kiss on the cheek that had been turned away. It was at that precise moment that without knocking Billy came bursting into the room. Conrad straightened up, turned and smiled at his brother. Then firmly leading him to the door by the shoulder he said –

"Come along Billy, we have to go. Haik has been working very hard and needs some rest."

Chapter 13

The role of an elder brother

Although in this particular year, Vahan had decided not to bring his family to Istanbul for the summer, his father Garabed had again hired the large house and garden in Suadiye as he had been doing for so many years. Ara, now married, had two little girls and had turned up for the summer from Cairo as usual. The whole Asadourian household trooped down to Suadiye during July and August. The sea there was not very attractive and no one went swimming, but there was a small sandy beach to which the little ones could go, and the gardens of the house itself were extensive. There was a substantial vineyard at the far end, fruit trees of all kinds were dotted about, there were several cultivated rows of different berries and all sorts of other exciting things.

Garabed invited Olga with her two boys to come and stay for a few days. The invitation was of course extended to all of the Avakians. Seta came with them but Natalie stayed with her grandmother Armineh. Suadiye was the next to last station on the ferry which ran down the Asian side from Uskudar – the last station, one further on at that time, was Pendig. Garabed and Ara went to work every morning by taking the ferry up to Uskudar. There they changed and took one of the frequent fast ferries which went from Uskudar to the Galata bridge on the European side, going up to their offices on the Tunel leading up to Pera. It was cumbersome and a little time-consuming but they went early and it did mean that they could all eat together as a family when they got back in the afternoon.

Garabed's daughter, Satenig, was 23 years old. She had developed a great friendship with Seta after Nerissa had left for France. Nerissa, who had married her brother Vahan, had been instrumental in looking after her when she had first arrived into the family. There was a considerable discrepancy of age, Seta being about seven or eight years older than Satenig. But Seta had always been very young for her age. Satenig had always had a deep respect and love for Nerissa, who had helped her through the difficult transition she had gone through when Vahan had brought her back from her Turkish Anatolian home. That love had spilled over onto Seta after Nerissa had gone to France with Vahan.

Satenig now managed the Asadourian household, both in the family home just off Taksim square and whenever they all came to Suadiye for the summer. Both Nerissa and Ara's wife, the two daughters-in-law, when they came to Istanbul simply let her get on with it. So it was she who gave the orders to the various traders who came to the back door, it was she who picked out the fresh fish or bargained with the butcher. Due to the circumstances of her childhood Satenig did not speak Armenian very well. Garabed too, coming from Kayseri and born well before the Armenian renaissance of the late Nineteenth Century, could speak no Armenian at all. Accordingly the talk at Suadiye was generally in Turkish. However, like all Bolsetsi, whether Jew, Greek or Armenian, people instinctively and naturally turned to other languages whenever it became necessary. The arrival of the two Avakian sisters and the two Bridgeman boys immediately brought English into the equation, though there remained, as always, a babel of languages round the dining table.

Meanwhile, the escalating European crisis had kept Harry at his desk at the Admiralty and he was not now due to come out until the 20th August. The whole family were then booked to return to London on the Simplon-Orient on the 15th September.

Conrad would occasionally go into Istanbul with the Asadourian men in the mornings. He would spend the day wandering round the city, exploring all the nooks and crannies of the town, sitting unobtrusively in the courtyard of the great mosques, imbibing all the art and the history of this pearl of civilisation. One day he met Haik by arrangement and they walked the whole length of the great Theodosian walls of the city, from the Blachernae Palace at the Golden Horn end right down to the Marmara sea and the fortress of Yedikule. They inspected every detail and stood and contemplated the spot where the Ottomans had finally breached the walls and broken into the city. They imagined that they had pinpointed exactly where it was that the last Byzantine Emperor Constantine had met his death. Conrad never lost this first love of Byzantine and medieval art.

On another day, he went for a long walk in the wooded hills behind Suadiye with his Aunt Seta and his cousin Satenig. Satenig was also no classic beauty, but like Seta she had a lively enthusiasm, which, coupled to the daring shorts that she wore for the expedition, aroused Conrad all over again. His sexual fantasies now transferred themselves onto the curvaceous charms of Satenig in place of those of his Aunt. Seta was a complete innocent in these matters and had no idea at all of having any effect on her nephew, who was after all fourteen years younger than her. But Satenig, only seven years or so older and of course completed unrelated to him, was far more aware in this field and knew perfectly well the effect she sometimes had on the young man.

The Asadourians had a large red Studebaker with a chauffeur to go with it. Ara loved driving it on Sundays when the whole household sometimes went into the hills for a picnic. This entailed a whole fleet of cars, specially hired for the purpose, to take all the servants and the food and the hangers-on. It also entailed filling up two great straw panniers holding huge glass containers with clear fresh water, from one or other of the famous springs and streams in the area; water sources, some of which were even referred to by name in classical Greek literature. Everyone had their own particular favourite and the arguments as to where they would stop and fill up on 'this' particular day went on each time.

In front of the Suadiye house was a large oval dusty space; a sort of cul-de-sac piazza. It had three large houses fronting onto it, with the fourth side being the earthen road leading gently downhill to the village and the ferry station. Ara, to the great alarm of Simone the chauffeur, would let Conrad drive the Studebaker round this spot, teaching him how to turn and brake and double-de-clutch. Billy would squat by the ornamental gate, always kept open, chewing blades of grass and watching. Conrad was gentle and kind to Ara's two little girls and would take them down to play on the little sandy beach. Billy would accompany them, but he was at the age when he had little patience dealing with three and four year-old girls. It has to be added that he did not have Conrad's natural kindness and tolerance either.

In one of the other two houses grouped round the piazza there was a Turkish family which included two boys one just 10 years-old and the other not quite 11. Billy was not allowed out of the front gate on his own, and would sit rather disconsolately by the iron gates and watch those two boys as they kicked a ball around the dusty square. On the second day, they came over and talked to him. However, as they knew no English and Billy knew not a word of Turkish, it did not get very far. They tried again on the next day, ending with them grinning at him and running off, shaking their heads and muttering good-humouredly about 'giavours'.

The moment inevitably came when Billy disobeyed and joined them in the dusty square, running with them into their own much smaller garden, and inviting them into his own. They remained without any common language and in fairness it should be added that the two older boys had no idea that Billy was only 7 years-old. The three of them got more and more daring, and eventually Billy was going with them down the road to the village and the ferry station to watch all the comings and goings of the ferries and the traffic along the coast road. He was always careful to be back in good time before he could be missed.

The two 10 year-old neighbours were not vicious or manipulative, they were simply mischievous and at an age when they wanted to dare to be naughty. It was probable that they too were not really allowed to go out of the square and down to the village. By the side of the ferry station, on the sea side of the coast road there was a regular daily market stall run by an elderly Greek grocer selling fresh fruit and vegetables. The fruit in bright colours was laid out very temptingly in attractive pyramids and the boys coveted the big red apples. The day came when by miming and making their intentions clear they persuaded Billy to join them in grabbing one of the apples and running.

What was Billy thinking about? His father was strict about this sort of thing and he was perfectly aware that it was wrong. Was it so as not to be outdone? Was it to act like other 10 year-olds and not to be ashamed, or thought a coward before these new friends? Whatever the reason, he nodded, and the three boys made a bungled dash for the fruit, grabbed an apple each and ran back across the street. But standing alongside the elderly Greek grocer on this particular day was his 19 year-old son who had come to help. Billy was the last to take an apple – he was the last to turn and run – and his little legs could not begin to keep up with the other boys. He scarcely reached the other side of the road when he was grabbed and held tightly by the young man, who had had no difficulty in chasing after him and catching him. He was then hauled back to the stall which stood by the exit of the ferry station.

As it happened, Conrad had just come back from one of his excursions into the city and was getting off the ferry. He witnessed the whole thing, and ran across immediately, as he saw Billy being unceremoniously led back across the street with the red apple still in his hand. Billy was white with fear but not at that point in tears. He was so frightened that he could not even cry. But when he saw Conrad running up he did start crying – tears more of relief than of fear.

Conrad came and quickly took the apple out of his brother's hand. He stammered in a mixture of pidgin Turkish and good French that he was the brother of the miscreant; that he was deeply sorry about what had happened; that the boy would be punished and that he Conrad would now pay handsomely for the damage. In order to emphasise the latter point Conrad produced a wad of money. This then began a rather one-sided argument with the irate stallholder and his equally angry son. The shouting on their part was in Turkish and Greek – with a mixture of bad French and even poorer English, when it became clear that Conrad was not understanding much of what was being said. As happened often in Istanbul in these sorts of street altercations, bystanders immediately gathered and stood about making ribald and unhelpful comments – most of them recommending that Billy should be given a good thrashing either there and then, or when the police were called. At one point the old Greek grocer became very angry and struck Conrad across the face. Conrad did not flinch, instead once again proffering the apple and holding out the money. When the young man raised his hand and also struck a blow with his fist on his nose, again Conrad did not move a muscle save to wipe away the flowing blood. But then the young man raised a hand to give Billy a cuff across his head. This time Conrad's hand shot out fast and he held the young man's hand still in a strong iron grip.

At this, the old man nodded at his son who for the first time let go of Billy's shoulder. Billy had all this time been clinging on desperately to

Conrad's legs. The situation calmed and the old man took the money Conrad had been holding out. He refused to take back the apple. He shook his head sorrowfully several times and made it clear to Conrad that the little boy should be severely punished by his father. Conrad said nothing more though he understood exactly what the old man was suggesting.

He turned to go, leading Billy across the road holding onto his shoulder. On the other side he let go of Billy's shoulder and still holding the apple he began walking through the village and up the dusty street leading back home. He walked fast, refusing to take Billy's hand. Billy had to trot alongside to keep up with him. His tears began again, but now no longer tears of fear but of guilt. He desperately wanted Conrad to smack him hard like his mother would have done, but Conrad simply strode on, ignoring him. They had not yet reached the little square when Billy stopped still and would not go a step farther. Billy, head down and still in tears said in a tremulous but clear voice –

"Are you going to tell Daddy when he comes?"

Conrad turned and looked down at his brother. His own nose was bleeding and he took out his handkerchief to stem the flow. He said –

"Don't be silly, of course not. But Billy you must know that what you did wasn't just naughty – don't you? That man has a family to feed – he has to sell his fruit so that he can earn a living. You were lucky that he didn't call the police"

Conrad looked at the apple he was still holding. Then with a huge swing he threw it far out into the small copse of trees alongside the road. He then took Billy's hand and they walked back to the house. Even though he was only seven, Billy knew that his brother had taken the slap and the hard punch that should have been administered to him.

Chapter 14

Countdown to war

The original plan was that Harry would join the rest of the family sometime during the first week in August. However pressure of work kept him at his desk at the Admiralty as the Polish crisis developed. Whatever happened in continental Europe the Royal Navy was not going to be caught unready. Naval Intelligence diligently plotted the position of almost every ship in the German Navy. The ticket that he had bought for himself had to be returned and there was even some question as to whether he could go at all.

But then the moment arrived when Harry felt that he had to make the effort to get away. He was now beginning to worry about his family stuck in Istanbul. There seemed to be little doubt that if Hitler persisted in his wish to attack Poland, it was likely that there would be war. He was of course unable to predict precisely where or when it would arise. But certainly if war was declared while his wife and children were still in Istanbul, they would be very vulnerable.

In the end his superiors agreed to let him go but insisted that he should go as far as he could by air and to get back as soon as he could. A seat was found for him on Imperial Airways leaving from Croydon airport. By a series of hops from London to Paris, then to Milan, and from there to Belgrade he finally got to Istanbul by train on the 20th August. By then Olga and the boys had returned to Makrikoy from their stay at Suadiye. Telegrams to Karekin's office had kept everyone fully aware of his movements and, on the day of his arrival, the whole family went down the road to Cobancesme station and took the train into town. It was a gorgeous sunny day as indeed it had been throughout Europe during the most of this August.

Harry's train was dead on time and, once again, he had the experience of arriving at Sirkedji station – an arrival which he had enjoyed so often since that first occasion 20 years ago. All the fuss and excitement; the porters jostling for custom with their two-wheel trolleys at the ready; the shaded restaurant on platform 1 with the unmistakeable aroma of Turkish coffee; the whistles and the excited calls of welcome; the steam engine steaming and hissing away at the front of the train as the travellers walked down the platform; the feeling of at last arriving at the gateway to the Orient. There were only three stations in Europe which had quite that same atmosphere. One was the Gare St Charles in Marseille. As you walked out of the station you stood at the top of wide marble steps which swept down to the city below and the Mediterranean in the distance, which seemed to be the gateway to Africa. Then there was the Stazione Centrale in Milan, which seemed to be the hub for so many destinations all over Europe. Then finally the much more modest Sirkedji station – but nevertheless the gateway to Asia and the whole of the East. All this, added to the exuberant welcome of his very own family, momentarily overwhelmed Harry with joy. It was a sublime moment for him, to be remembered all his life.

But the crisis in Europe was on everyone's mind, except of course that of Billy, whose excitement at his father's arrival was entirely over the top for a little English boy, but was probably fairly restrained for a little Armenian boy. For some days after Harry's arrival everyone carefully scanned the newspapers, whilst Karekin kept his ears open for all the gossip and the news amongst his business circles. The family had tickets booked on the Simplon-Orient express leaving on the 12th September, but there were worries that the crisis seemed to be developing faster than originally thought.

Meanwhile as the summer wore on, in Paris Hakim sat his exams and appeared to have done reasonably well, The usual parental worries where exams are concerned had been completely subsumed by the increasing crisis in Europe which was on everybody's mind. Like almost everyone else, Vahan and Nerissa perused every newspaper, and listened to every rumour, as the summer days passed. No one really knew what war was going to mean in these coming days of airpower. The catchphrase –'The bomber will always get through' was on everyone's mind, and the atmosphere of anxiety pervaded every home in Europe.

Then, on the 22nd August, came the news of the flight by Ribbentrop to Moscow to negotiate with the arch-enemy of the Germans – Stalin. This was almost immediately followed by the bombshell news of the signing by Ribbentrop and Molotov of the Nazi-Soviet Pact. Nazi Germany and Soviet Russia had been trading vicious insults against each other for the last six years but had now come to an agreement. Officially referred to as a Non-Aggression Pact, it was clear to Vahan, and to most intelligent observers, that it was basically an agreement to bring about a fourth Partition of Poland – and arguably the most immoral of all of them.

It has always remained unclear as to which of the two dictators, Hitler or Stalin, most loathed entering into the arrangement. But for both of them there were clear and immediate benefits. For Hitler, it was part of his 'one at a time' strategy. He was delighted at the outcome. He could now deal with Poland exactly as he wished. He became quite certain that the British and French would now back out of their obligations to Poland as they had in the case of Czechoslovakia. After all, as he saw it, if the Western states had backed out of its obligations to a far more defensible country with a stable democratic government, surely they would not now rush into war for a country with a government as autocratic as Germany's, and which they could no longer hope to help in any significant way.

For Stalin it was a chance to push westwards the frontiers of the Soviet Union, thus keeping the German army that much further away from the Soviet heartlands. He was more perceptive and better informed than Hitler, and saw that the western democracies would probably fight this time and a nice long war between Great Britain and France on the one hand and Nazi Germany on the other suited him very well.

The Admiralty was put on alert; letters were written to the Dominion governments warning them of the imminence of war; preparations for the fleet to move to Scapa Flow were made; even from a distance Harry was fully aware of these developments. Harry now felt that he had to make great efforts to get his family away sooner than anticipated. He began going down daily to Sirkedji station, often taking one of the children with him, to try and get tickets for the journey back to London. Each day passed with the political crisis worsening, but he could not find any spare places on the train. Everybody was on the move – German students returning to Vienna – Italians anxious to get back to Milan – French businessmen in a hurry to return to Paris. Not a ticket was to be had.

He was now under a lot of stress. Karekin and Armineh kept suggesting that Turkey was probably a safer place for his family to be. Karekin never went so far as to suggest that Harry too should stay put, but he did point out that Turkey was going to remain neutral this time and would not suffer the aerial bombardment that London was sure to face. His suggestion was that Harry could return on his own without bothering about a sleeper. If war did not break out, Olga and the children could return on the tickets they still had. But if war prevented them so doing, as Olga had been born an Ottoman subject, she would not be in any difficulty, being a neutral.

"Neutral – but for how long," replied Harry. "It might be all very well for Olga, but my children are all British subjects. No way, Karekin, no way. I don't know how you can suggest such a thing. My God, what do you think is going to happen to the remaining Armenians here if Turkey does eventually join the war on the German side as she did last time. No, we must all leave and we must go now if we can. If I can't get train tickets we must think of taking a boat to Alexandria. We should be able to get home from Egypt easily after that."

"Very well," replied Karekin. "You might well be right, but I think that you can afford to wait for your booking on the 12th. You can always fall back on the ship idea if anything happens before then. Look, your Prime Minister isn't going to go to war for Danzig or even for Poland as a whole. Consider what happened last year at Munich – you'll see – you can certainly wait until the 12th – Mr. Chamberlain will dither and that will be the end of it."

Harry shook his head sadly.

"I fear that might indeed be a possibility, but I

have to act on the basis that such a moral surrender will not happen this time."

In the interest of objectivity, it would be fair to add at this stage a fact that neither Karekin nor Harry knew, namely that Chamberlain, despite what had happened at Munich, had in fact written a letter on this very same day to Hitler. This letter, with all its historical resonance, must absolve the man from some of the worse strictures hurled at him by people and historians writing in hindsight. After referring to the recent conclusion of the German-Soviet agreement his letter went on –

"This agreement seems to be taken to indicate that intervention by Great Britain on behalf of Poland need no longer be reckoned with. No greater mistake could be made. Whatever the nature of that agreement, it cannot alter Great Britain's obligation to Poland which we have stated repeatedly and plainly in public.

It has been alleged that if His Majesty's government had made their position more clear in 1914 that great catastrophe could have been avoided. Whether or not there is any force in that allegation the present government is resolved that on this occasion there shall be no such misunderstanding."

The letter concluded by making it clear that war would inevitably follow if an invasion of Poland took place. A fairly clear statement it would seem; but Hitler simply did not believe it. He believed that Chamberlain was bluffing and that he would never actually take the step to start a war in the circumstances now facing him.

Chapter 15

Family trivia drowning out world crisis

B illy was well aware that there was a crisis in the air after his father arrived. It was not just that all the adults around him were arguing. In his grandfather Karekin's house in Makrikoy everyone always argued. It was the Avakian way and even at the age of seven he recognised how different it was than back home in London. Nothing was ever taken as 'the gospel truth'. It was not just one's right to question, but almost your duty to question – and that applied to everyone, even the children, though not perhaps to Billy, who was excused a lot by his doting grandfather.

Within a day or two of Harry's arrival he began going down in the morning to the station at the bottom of the hill, often taking Conrad with him. Everyone knew that he was trying to get earlier tickets for the family all to go home right away, rather than waiting for their booked return which was not due for a couple of weeks yet. Billy was not insensitive to atmosphere; he understood the adult tension and anxiety, but he really did not understand what it was actually all about.

For most children, until they learn better, the world tends to be all about them, and to revolve entirely round their problems. This applied even more than most to the self-centred Billy, always indulged by everyone around him except his father.

In fact, believing as he did that the only thing his parents ever seriously thought about was himself, he came to the conclusion that at least some of their tension was due to their anger involving him, because of an incident that had taken place shortly after his father's arrival. In the great open front room of Karekin's house was a low glass-fronted cupboard against the wall near the front door. This contained a wonderful bright red fire engine. It had ladders that went up and down, four resplendent firemen sitting at the sides and great rubber wheels. It was a wondrous toy that had belonged in the dim and distant past to the dead Haik, who if he had survived would have been the boy's uncle. Billy was only allowed to look at it and even to open the glass door and touch it, but not to take it out.

He had rather boldly begun to go a little further on each occasion and was soon taking it out and pushing it along the floor – working the ladders on the roof, picking off the firemen and putting them into new positions. Inevitably the moment came when he broke one of the firemen. He stepped on its head when it fell off as he was pushing the engine along. Billy could never recall anything of the talk of war, but all his life he recalled vividly that feeling of complete panic as he stood helplessly looking down at the broken figure.

His tears, which tended to flow rather easily when he was 6 began to stream silently. Almost as if he had willed it the first on the scene coming down the stairs was Conrad with Haik behind him, both laughing and giggling about something. Conrad took in the situation at once. With Haik's help he picked up the red fire engine and they bundled it back into the glass case. He held onto the broken fireman which he slipped into his pocket. As it was nearly lunchtime other adults were coming in from the garden and the sitting room.

Billy remained fairly miserable and in a state of fear as the family finally sat down at the table. As the conversation flowed Conrad turned and said to Harry, who had earlier returned from yet another fruitless trip to Sirkedji station –

"Oh, Dad, I'm afraid we have broken one of the firemen on that fire engine in the Hall. His head came off when we took it out to look at it. I'm sure all it needs is some glue."

Lunch progressed as Billy in a state of inchoate guilt said nothing. But what neither Billy nor Conrad knew was that Armineh, the boy's awesome grandmother, of whom Billy was a little afraid, had witnessed the whole thing from behind the stairs where she had been seeing to the table. After allowing the conversation to go on a little, she said very deliberately to Billy at a moment when there was, for once, a slight hush amongst the clamour of an Avakian lunch.

"Is that really right Billy, what Conrad and Haik have just said about the broken fireman?"

Suddenly there was a silence as everyone

turned to look at the seven year-old. Billy flushed bright red and saw his grandfather – Karekin – who had always been particularly kind to him, looking at him with a trusting look of confidence that saved the boy from just nodding which had been his first thought. Instead, knowing that above all else he must not start crying, he mumbled –

"No Grandma, I'm sorry, it was me who broke the fireman."

Harry said sharply –

"Billy did you take it out of the glass cage."

"Yes Daddy – I'm sorry."

"Well that was very naughty. No more lunch for you my lad – go and stand in the corner over there with your hands on your head, and stay there till we finish."

Punishment from Billy's parents was usually swift and sure. Olga smacked him often when she was angry and in front of anyone. His father never ever struck him in front of any third party – but he did smack him usually across the back of his legs if they were alone. At no time did his father ever raise his hand to either Conrad or Natalie.

Billy was always aware from a very early age that his father was far more severe with him than he was with Conrad. It never bothered him. For a start, Conrad was nearly 9 years older and never appeared to get into any trouble, as seemed to be Billy's lot in life. Even when he did get into trouble Harry never once ever raised his hand against him. On one occasion when Billy was 4 and Conrad was about 12 he did get into some trouble with a neighbour lad whose mother then reported him to Olga. She grabbed hold of him and said she was going to report him to his father when he got home. Conrad was terrified and went to his room and sat on the edge of his bed looking down at the floor. Billy remembered going and sitting next to him to try clumsily to comfort him, but he didn't respond. Olga remonstrated with Harry later that he had not punished Conrad as he should have done. His reply was –

"Olga, hokis, I could see that simply being reported to me was punishment enough for the boy."

Billy, on the other hand, would receive smacks from his mother, and then if reported to his father would even occasionally feel his slipper as well as his hand. The smack was nearly always purely nominal. Nevertheless he always ran on these occasions to be comforted by Conrad, who never failed to take time off to talk to him and give him a cuddle, however busy he was. It was almost as if he too knew that Billy received much more punishment than he did.

Billy stood in that corner for the rest of lunch. Once everyone had finished and were leaving the table Olga called out –

"You can come out now Billy."

He was a bit sulky by then as everyone went out to have coffee in the garden. Conrad had kept some fruit for him, which he quietly gave him when he came out into the garden. Billy took them as if it was his right. Needless to say within a few minutes he had forgotten the whole incident.

However, that night before going to bed, as he was about to go into his parent's room, already in his pyjamas, to kiss them goodnight, he overheard a short snatch of conversation between them which brought up the whole incident again in his mind. They were dressing for dinner – guests were coming later – and as he stood at their door prior to knocking to go in, he heard Olga say to his father –

"Harry, darling, you were a bit hard on Billy this afternoon weren't you? In the corner for almost an hour in front of everyone."

"My love I don't really care how naughty he may be – naughty is what little boys can be, and a smack or a reprimand is all that is usually needed. But being a bit sly and letting Conrad take the blame – that's different and needs a different level of punishment. If I catch him at it again, he'll get a good walloping. Now if…"

At that point Billy knocked and went in. He kissed them and received his normal warm welcome and hugs from both. But for the rest of the few days left of peace, it was not the coming war which was on Billy's mind – but the red fire engine. So for Billy this was not the week of the countdown to war, but the week of the headless fireman. Even then and even at that young age, it was already fast becoming a narrative that Billy was creating as part of his own sense of identity.

Chapter 16

The last train home

It was only two days later that Harry with Conrad in tow came back somewhat breathlessly from the morning visit to Sirkedji station. Harry was calling out even as he came in at the front door.

"We're going! Olga can you hear me up there – we're going right now. I have got us a four-berth cabin for this afternoon and we are leaving right now – now. The tickets are for the 2.00pm train this afternoon."

Olga came out of their bedroom and leaning down over the balustrade called out –

"Harry darling we simply won't be able to make it. I can't get everything packed and ready in time. How can we get all the trunks to the station in time."

"Hokis, we have no choice. I absolutely insist. We are leaving and going on that train. They are the only tickets available and I was lucky to get them"

By now the whole household was out of their rooms, each adding their ideas and anxieties. Karekin came out of his study shaking his head and remonstrating with Harry. But Harry kept his nerve; even with all his in-laws pressurising him, he held firm. Billy was in the hall, playing carefully with the red fire engine. His grandmother had, after the incident when he had been made to stand in the corner for an hour, changed the rules and had said that Billy could take it out and play with it if he was careful. As Conrad and Harry had rushed in he had stopped playing, had put the engine away carefully and watched as his father insisted on an immediate departure

He always remembered later, with a sort of deep pride, his father standing up, against all the pressure being put on him by his in-laws and particularly all the women, quietly and with firm conviction. But then perhaps even at that moment, Billy was beginning to fashion the narrative which would be with him all his life.

When it became clear that, come what may, the family would be leaving that very morning, Conrad grabbed Billy and pulled him upstairs to help him get ready – to sort out with him the toys he could take with him and those he would have to leave behind. Olga began throwing things into the trunks. Two cars were hired to drive to the station and were ordered to come at once so that loading could begin. Telephone calls went all round Bolis warning everybody that the Bridgemans were leaving on that day's Simplon-Orient. The two hired cars arrived and stood in the road receiving case after case as they were packed and brought down. The Asadourian Studebaker turned up driven by Ara and with Satenig inside – others had gone direct to Sirkedji.

Everyone was aware that the reason for the hurried departure of the British family was the

rumours of the coming war. Armenian goodbyes tend to drag on and be an occasion for an
outpouring of emotion in any case, but in these
circumstances the emotion was even stronger. All
thinking people throughout Europe had an exaggerated fear of what bombing was going to do
to cities like London. So the tears and the kisses
and the farewells had an added drama due to
the feeling that this might really be the last time.
Time passed and as everyone got ready there was
a clear possibility that they might not make it. It
was the 30th August and meanwhile on that very
day Hitler confirmed his orders for the invasion
of Poland to commence in twenty-four hours.

Other well-wishers' cars began arriving at the
front door. There was an atmosphere of controlled panic and about this time Billy began
to get a little frightened. The sight of all those
adults, who until then represented bedrock for
him, acting panicky and a bit hysterical, was un-
nerving. But in the middle of it all standing like a
rock talking quietly with Karekin, who was himself now calm and rocklike, stood his cool father,
and that sight calmed his childish fears. Of course
he was far too little to realise that they could both
afford to be so calm because they both knew that
in the long run their respective spouses, Olga and
her mother Armineh, despite all the expostula-
tions and suppressed panic, were actually getting
all the real work efficiently completed.

It was getting late when Billy was bundled into
the first car together with Conrad and Olga. They

drove at considerable speed along the Marmara coast road and through the great Theodosian walls by the side of the railway line and over the hill and up to the front entrance of Sirkedji station. Here it was all hustle and bustle as they went through the great chandeliered hall and onto the platform. The train was standing, hissing and steaming alongside platform 1. The coach which went all the way to London Victoria was at the far end.

Harry and the car driven by Ara arrived, closely followed by the second hired car. Three porters were hurriedly engaged and the whole family began hurrying down the platform alongside the train. The noise, the whistles and the shouting, was deafening. Billy could see his father and mother striding along in front with Natalie alongside them, looking at all the coaches seeking for the number of the one booked that morning. Young men were all leaning out of the windows laughing and joking. Billy, having to trot to keep up, was holding on tight to Conrad's hand as he was hurrying along. But Conrad was holding back in order to keep pace with the two porters and all the luggage.

"Madam, monsieur, the train is about to leave, you must get on board," called out one of the railway officials, giving a great blast on his whistle.

More whistles and shouts grew louder and the train gave a sort of lurch. Harry turned round and shouted at Conrad at the top of his voice–

"Conrad – get Billy onto the train – there –

there in that coach where you are now – now."

He himself was far in front helping Olga and Natalie onto the train about 3 coaches away. The three porters, already well paid by Harry, were passing up all the trunks and cases into the hands of all those laughing young men who had been leaning out of the windows. They were grabbing the cases as they were handed up and setting them down in the corridor in which they were all standing. The steps up to the carriage door were steep and Conrad lifted Billy up as he tried to scramble up and swung him onto the carriage floor. He then clambered up after him, and one of the station guards who had been whistling, shouting and waving his green flag came running up and shut the door as Conrad got in. The train give a great lurch again and began slowly gliding past the platform and on its way.

The only berth Harry had managed to get was a four-berth cabin – not the usual two berths with a bathroom in between. On each of the three nights the family spent on their way home the brown-suited attendant brought them a thin mattress when he came to prepare the beds. This mattress was then laid on the floor of the compartment. Natalie and Olga slept on the top berths and Harry and Conrad slept on the two bottom ones, while Billy would bed down on the mattress on the floor in between. On each day Conrad would remonstrate, but Harry would insist that it was Billy who had to sleep on the floor. Harry had managed to get hold of this last-minute cancelled berth by assuring everybody that his youngest son was under five and could sleep with his mother. The thin mattress was simply an additional service provided by the coach attendant in exchange for a very generous present.

The others could all read with their little reading lights above each bunk. Billy would drop off to sleep long before all the lights went out. However, every night – half asleep – he would feel himself being picked up by Conrad and gently put down on the bunk with him pushed up against the wall, and this is how he would wake up in the morning with Conrad's arms over him. Harry saw this every day – but next night it was the same – Billy would start up on the floor.

Three days went by. The train rumbled its way through the Balkans and into Italy. The family passed through Paris and onto the night ferry – and eventually onto Platform 1 of London Victoria station in the early morning of the 3rd September 1939. All five of them, even including Harry, felt a sense of security and calm, after all the travelling and excitement, as they entered the sitting room of their home. They were just in time to settle down rather solemnly in the sitting room to listen to the radio. It was rare for all five of them to sit together to listen to a programme. Billy would sit with his mother to listen to Childrens' Hour, and Conrad and Harry would sometimes listen to things together. But this occasion stood out as something different. All five were sitting together to listen to something on the wireless. It was Chamberlain announcing in his dour and rather bland tones that "consequently this country is now at war with Germany."

Chapter 17

The declaration of war

The signing of the Nazi-Soviet Pact had of course alerted the British and French governments to the immediate possibility of a German invasion of Poland. Chamberlain summoned Parliament and in the chamber he reiterated that the British commitments to the defence of Poland would be honoured. But the speech was not very inspiring and did not arouse any enthusiasm. The mood of the House of Commons itself was quite different from the days before the sell-out of Munich. Members of all parties were keenly watching out for any signs of weakness on the part of the government. In France too, despite every effort of that arch-appeaser the foreign minister – Bonnet – to delay any sharp response, both Daladier and the rest of the cabinet were resolved not to back down this time.

Hitler had originally given the order for his armies to invade and march into Poland on the 26th August. But a series of reports coming in – Chamberlain's supposed firmness – the signing of yet another Anglo-Polish treaty - the decision, passed on to Hitler that afternoon, that Mussolini intended to remain neutral for the time being – all gave Hitler an attack of nerves. At the very last moment he decided to call off the troops, while he looked for other ways to see if he could prevent British intervention.

Hitler had now publicly held back from a war which he clearly wanted. Everyone who mattered in Europe, went away with all sorts of wrong messages. The appeasers, the two foreign ministers – Lord Halifax and Bonnet - thought there might yet be a possibility of again negotiating out of the dilemma. The stalwarts nodded their collective heads commenting that that proved that all that was ever needed was to stand firm and the man would back down. The Poles remained clear in their own minds that the one thing they would not do is to go cap-in-hand to Berlin and be bullied into any sort of capitulation like so many others.

Everyone knew that the invasion had been called off when Hitler made an offer of another conference, with pre-conditions. It now took three days for the British foreign office to compile their all-important reply to the offer. It was worded extremely carefully – leaving the door open for further negotiations, but not retreating an inch from the commitment to Poland. This resulted in a series of wild and angry confrontations between Henderson, the weak British ambassador in Berlin, and Ribbentrop the German foreign minister. Finally at midday on the 31st August, Hitler, now insisting that when it came to the crunch the British would do nothing, ordered the invasion to commence on the morning of the next day – the 1st September. From the early hours of that day the German Juggernaut poured into Poland.

So did Britain and France not immediately draw its collective sword in a great rush of honourable defiance? Not a bit of it! A combination of Mussolini's weasel words, the pusillanimous pacifism of Bonnet trying every tactic short of actually repudiating the guarantee to wriggle out of it, and the pressures building up on Chamberlain all through the 1st and 2nd of September delayed what should have been an immediate response. Parliament waited for Chamberlain to arrive on the 2nd and he finally rose to speak at about 8.00pm. He spoke for only four minutes – made no mention of any ultimatum or any declaration of war and evoked not a single response from anyone in the whole chamber, where everyone looked on in stunned silence as he sat down

Then at last the leader of the Labour Opposition – Arthur Greenwood deputising for Clement Attlee who was ill at the time – rose to speak. This was the famous moment when Leo Amery, a Conservative MP, sitting right behind Chamberlain, called out –"Speak for England, Arthur". Greenwood rose to the occasion and delivered a stinging rebuke which left Chamberlain shattered. Already German troops had been rampaging for two days through the borderlands of Poland, and Warsaw had been bombed all day on both days. Chamberlain's delay has always been blamed on the baleful influence of the insidious Bonnet, permanently on the telephone to everyone. Whilst in hindsight it was unlikely that he was ever going to fall into the trap of another Munich, nevertheless to the very last minute he appeared to be hesitating.

The ultimatum, finally sent at 9.00am on the 3rd September, was timed to expire at 11.00am. At 11.10 the British Embassy in Berlin telephoned to say that there had been no response. At 11.15 Chamberlain prepared to make his broadcast in the special studio the BBC had set up for him an hour before. This was the broadcast that the Bridgeman family listened to on the very morning of their return to London. This was the broadcast that everyone over the age of six at the time claims to remember, although they are probably only remembering the countless replays put out by the BBC on every conceivable anniversary.

In the end it took only a week for the truth gradually to become clear to the Polish leaders - that Britain and France had never intended to fight in any significant way in their defence. The ironic truth of the matter was that Poland was as much betrayed by the Anglo-French declaration of war as the Czechs had been betrayed by their declaration of peace.

Chapter 18

Vichy France – the start

It is one of the features of almost all military commanders of any country and any age, that when things go well and their armies are successful, all the credit goes to the quality of leadership that had been shown. But when things go badly and the defeat of their armies loom, it is the instinct of almost every officer corps in every country to shift the blame onto the civilian leaders and politicians. They will be accused of not backing them up sufficiently. Where that is obviously not possible, as in the case of Ludendorff facing defeat in the Great War, they will arrange for the armistice, the surrender, or whatever humiliation is to be imposed, to be left to the civilians – as if the military had had nothing to do with it.

So again it was in France in June 1940, as the country reeled from the greatest and most humiliating military disaster in its whole history. The consequences of this military defeat were devastating. Half the country was occupied by foreign troops. In the south, in the part that was unoccupied, a shabby right-wing authoritarian regime under Marshal Petain was set up with its capital in the fashionable spa town of Vichy, chosen largely because it had so many large hotels able to accommodate all the government staff and general hangers-on that flocked into the town.

One of the few virtues of the concept of the modern nation-state is that it can give rise to a strong and single-minded patriotic fervour in the majority of the people. However, the obverse side of this virtue is that the defeat of its single-nation armies will be an even more terrible catastrophe than would be the case in a multi-national empire. The defeat becomes a supreme catastrophe and will create a trauma in everyone, right or left, rich or poor. It will cause an all-embracing despair and a collapse of self-confidence that will permeate the whole of society.

So it was in the extraordinary rapidity of the fall of France in June 1940. The one solid rock on which everyone in Europe was counting on, including Stalin, had been the French army, yet the Germans had treated it with the same contempt they had shown to the Polish army only a few months before. The search for scapegoats began immediately. The Catholic Right, now in the ascendant, was quite clear - it had all been due to the deep moral decadence of the Third Republic, particularly in the previous four years. The Stavisky scandals of 1936, the Popular Front government of Leon Blum, the decline of patriotism and the pernicious influence of the Jews – it was all so clear to the French Catholic elite. Everything they disliked about modern French society was blamed, Even the writings of literary figures like Proust, Gide or Cocteau were quoted as having given rise to the moral decadence which was the cause of the great catastrophe.

But the one thing they all ignored was that in essence this had been a totally straightforward and uncomplicated military defeat. Everything that happened stemmed from that, and no amount of talk about moral decadence or latent pacifism could disguise that clear fact. The officer class in France was Catholic, right-wing, and basically anti-republican, and this included Petain, Weygand and most of the rest of the generals. The idea that France was overwhelmed by a huge unstoppable German army with a vast superiority of men, tanks and guns, was simply untrue. The numbers of soldiers in the French and Allied armies were slightly more than that of the Germans. Contrary to the myth propagated by the defeated French generals, the French army had in fact been provided with as many tanks as the German, and some of them were even superior in quality to those of the Panzers.

The military collapse was the consequence of a failed military caste which had refused to keep up with the changes in the techniques of modern warfare. The myth that half the French conscript 'poilus' were drunk all the time is just that – a myth. The failure lay entirely in the military class which led the army. As always, the generals managed to make it appear that society was somehow at fault and not them.

The unhappy Third Republic had never had many admirers. The several administrations had followed each other with incredible speed. Daladier's first government in 1934 was frightened out of office after only eight days – a record even by the short-lived standards of the Third Republic. In the aftermath of the complete defeat of the country in the summer of 1940 there was a temptation to blame all those forces that had supported the Republic in its last days – Blum – the teachers – the workers – the socialists – the literary figures of Paris – they were all guilty of something. Sitting in a railway carriage on a short journey from the suburbs back into Paris shortly after the Armistice was announced, Vahan was harangued by an old gentleman sitting opposite him in the train, a retired officer sporting the rosette of the Legion d'Honneur, who kept saying that what had happened had served the country right.

"Everything that has happened my dear sir was all the fault of the Third Republic which had turned France into "La France babillarde" – a nation of aesthetes and chatterers. Just look at the way the Jews, the Freemasons and those self-serving parliamentary deputies cheated us."

Vahan said little, just listened to the man going on and on, trotting out all the tired old right-wing shibboleths. He reported all this to Nerissa when he got back home –

"My dear, I even got the impression that he was to an extent secretly pleased about the defeat. His attitude seemed to be one of 'now we can clear them all out.'"

Certainly the Third Republic was unstable, certainly it had lurched from one crisis to another, but in the end it never, at any stage approached anything near the abyss of immorality into which the right-wing Catholic elite allowed the French state to fall between 1940 and 1944.

The complete collapse of the French army in a matter of just a few weeks in May and June of 1940 came as much of a surprise to Vahan as it did to most Frenchmen at the time. But as an Armenian citizen of the Ottoman Empire who had survived the deportations and massacres of 1915, when the state had turned against a whole section of its own citizens, he was in many ways more able to cope with the disastrous consequences of the Occupation than many of his French friends and neighbours, for whom the defeat was intolerable.

Right from the start of the German occupation, interspersed with the harsh conditions of the lack of food and fuel, Paris fell into a febrile state of excitement and fear. The theatres, which re-opened soon after the Germans arrived in the city, were full to the brim. The cinemas flourished with an enormous cinematic output producing some of the best films of the whole French cinema. And amongst the audiences flocking to all that entertainment sat the blond and handsome German officers and soldiers – both those from the Wehrmacht and those from the SS.

Collaboration!!

A word with enormous overtones of emotion and passion; a word which described the full range of responses to the presence of an enemy occupier. What exactly constitutes 'collaboration' for the ordinary citizen? The two extremes at either end of the spectrum are simple – heroic resistance on the one hand or vicious supportive anti-semitism on the other. But what about the small everyday problems confronting the ordinary citizen? When in the crowded Metro a shy young German soldier, probably not more than nineteen years old, rises and offers his seat to a lady – is it collaboration if she quickly smiles at him and sits down. Or must she turn her back and ignore his polite purely human gesture and remain standing, whilst the young soldier stands in blushing confusion while everyone stares at the empty seat.

What about the moment when an elderly German Colonel, maybe even in the hated black uniform of the SS, is cycling along the fairly empty street. A little girl suddenly runs across the street right in front of him. In a desperate attempt to avoid hitting her he swerves and is knocked over by a passing car which hurries on its way. Several French men and women, each with all sorts of different political views, are passing nearby. All of them, without thinking, run to pick him up and make sure he is all right – one of them going to collect his bike and wheeling it back to him.

Collaboration?

The issue should not of course be exaggerated. Those politicians, intellectuals and philosophers on the Right, who had despised the Third Republic and who believed that France had lost the war because of an innate decadence, were certainly collaborators in the full sense of the word. They also believed that Germany had won the war, that it was only a matter of time, and that it would be best for France to position itself for the new order. They regularly painted images for the current position of the French relative to their German conquerors by metaphors of a sexual relationship in which France played the woman's role.

France was unique in all the conquered countries in the West in having retained a legitimate government intact. In Norway and Holland the legitimate governments had fled, whilst in Denmark, although the King remained, he ostentatiously paraded the fact that he was a prisoner, and far from collaborating was a thorn in the flesh of his German governors. Whatever De Gaulle might say in London, the government of Marshal Petain had clearly been the legally constituted government at the end of the Third Republic. When Reynaud resigned as Prime Minister as the Germans poured over the country, he advised the President, as was his constitutional right and indeed duty, to call on another Minister to form a new government. He advised the President to call on Petain, who was at the time the Minister of Defence, to attempt to form a new government. Accordingly Petain became the new Prime Minister, backed by Parliament. Had Reynaud fled to North Africa with as many of the Parliament and his ministers as would accompany him, it might have been different. But he did not and thus Vichy France came legitimately into being.

Vahan of course was a Turkish citizen lawfully on business in France with all the necessary visas, papers and rights of residence. He therefore had all the rights of a citizen of a neutral and, in the early stages, 'friendly' country. This of course also applied to Nerissa and Hakim, his adopted son. But Hakim was a Jew – furthermore a foreign Jew not a French Jew. There was nothing in the family passport to show this, but in addition to the family passport and visa there were their three identity papers – the Turkish nufus – on which were clearly marked 'Ermeni' and 'Yahudi' .

As he and Nerissa watched events unfold during the remainder of 1940 and the early months of 1941 it never crossed their mind that they might be some personal danger. Anti-semitism had been such a normal part of the French political scene in the late thirties that the arrival of the Germans seemed to make little difference. The same scurrilous newspapers continued to spew out the same virulent hatred and irrational prejudices, with perhaps just a touch of added smugness. It was not all that different in England. Anti-semitism was just as rife in the English upper and upper-middle classes during the thirties. What made the difference was the military defeat – a defeat entirely attributable to the inept, catholic, authoritarian officer class, not the 'poilus'.

Already on three occasions in the early months of 1941 the Germans, had rounded up some Jews in Paris with full French police cooperation, ostensibly as reprisals against Resistance attacks. These Jews were sent to temporary internment camps and were part of the first convoys that left for Auschwitz from Occupied France. The government in Vichy raised no objections to these arrests and eventually an arrangement was worked out between Laval in Vichy and the German authorities in Paris that a further 10,000 Jews were to be deported from the directly administered area of Vichy France - the Unoccupied Zone. Originally the Germans wanted to limit these early deportations to those aged between 18 and 40.. It was the Vichy French who proposed that the deportations should also include the children of those deported. Eichman, who had come to Paris for the express purpose of making the deal with the French, was surprised but accepted the proposal. Laval claimed that his suggestion was made to avoid families being separated. This was pure hypocrisy. It was just as hypocritical as the same requirement demanded by Father Tizso, the Catholic priest who was the leader of independent Slovakia created after Munich, who required that when the Jews were deported whole families should be sent away for 'Christian' reasons. What Vichy wanted to avoid above all was having to care for orphaned children after their parents had been deported.

The first really significant mass deportation from France began on the 16th July 1941 and it involved 9,000 French policemen. In two days of

mass arrests and round-ups, with the French police doing all the work, those unfortunate enough
to be on some list, amounting to about 14,000
Jews, including 4,000 children, were arrested In
Paris. Over half of these were crowded into the
Vel d'Hiver sports stadium where they remained
in indescribably squalid conditions for five or six
days – without any food or water before all being
deported to Auschwitz. Not a single German soldier was involved in this round-up.

A few weeks later, Vichy, without any prompt-
ing from the German authorities sent its own police into several towns in the unoccupied south
of the country and netted a further 7,000 Jews.
These were sent on to the squalid internment
camp of Drancy outside Paris.

On that morning of the 16th July, Vahan was
out and about in the streets of Paris and watched
as the French police arrested and led away family after family. As an Armenian, he understood
perfectly well what a government meant when it
used the word 'deportation'. Like everyone else
he really had no sure idea what was at the end of
the railway line for these deportees, but as an Armenian he could only look on in horror as he saw
the families being led away down the street with
a full comprehension of the likely consequence.
There they went, with their pathetic suitcases in
their hands and with their weeping, screaming
children holding on desperately with one hand
to some ragged doll and with the other dragging
on their mother's hand or, if none was available,

onto her skirt.

Not all the policemen were harsh or stony-faced. Vahan recounted that evening to Nerissa that he had seen a policeman carrying a suitcase in each hand and clearly in some personal distress. He was leading a group of children and old people, all carrying little bundles. Vahan followed this little group until it was joined by other groups all heading for the Vel d'Hiver sports stadium. Vahan saw that every group was led by a French policeman, or, where there was a large group, by several. When he got back to the apartment he found that Hakim was still at school. He told Nerissa –

"I felt terrible – how can they do it? Without the co-operation of all those gendarmes it just could not happen – no way – there simply aren't enough German police in France to carry out anything like this."

"But Vahan what is it all about?"

"I was outside one block when I saw one family come out being pushed by a couple of gendarmes who were shouting – 'Hurry up! Hurry up! Don't make us waste our time'. You know I was on the pavement right beside them. The group consisted of a woman and four children. There were two boys about 10 and 11 years old, a little girl – God I even heard her name – Annette, and a small boy. Can you believe it, the little girl said that she had left her comb behind and could she go and get it. One of the policemen said she could but that she had to return straight away. Do you know she did, and this time with a little doll in her hand."

"Oh Vahan!"

"Then – you won't believe this – in the melee of all those police and Jews, just as a couple of police busses came up to take them away, I saw the woman who was holding tight to her two little ones, Annette and the little boy, whisper to the two 10 and 11 year-old boys to run away – I was right beside her. Oh God, Nerissa my soul – they did as they were told and vanished into the watching crowd. The woman will probably never ever see them again."

"But Vahan, where are they all being sent – is it all that bad? I heard that…."

"No, no my soul, I don't know, but you can be sure that it's not just a nice agricultural area where they will all become happy farmers. We, above all, surely know, don't we, what 'deportation' usually means when applied by nation-state fanatics to any minority living in their midst. The Turks introduced the concept in 1915 and as a result a million Armenians died. No one, least of all the Jewish Zionist leaders, ever said a word, and as a result the same 'deportation' is being applied here and now."

"Oh my God, Vahan, what about Hakim?"

"No, no we really don't need to worry. He is our son and we are all Turkish citizens."

"But Vahan, my soul, everybody here knows he is adopted and is Jewish. You've heard how everyone is going round denouncing each other to the police and to the Germans."

"Hmm, you know that never crossed my mind – but you may be right. It certainly seems to be the case that the whole of French society seem to be writing letters of denunciation all the time. What the hell has happened to this basically tolerant and liberal people? God, our very own Concierge could be at it right now for all I know. Look, I think we should consider leaving Paris and the occupied Zone and going south to the Vichy-administered area. It should surely be safer for Hakim there."

"Oh, my soul, I don't know, I just don't know. At least here in Paris we are registered with the police. We've lived in this apartment for four years and our neighbours can vouch for us. If we just drift off to the south like so many others we may just end up as homeless refugees and foreigners to boot."

"No. no – I'm not suggesting for a moment a moonlight flit across the boundary between the two zones like those poor refugee Jews have to do. No, I'll get a proper Ausweis or whatever it is they call it. Remember, we do have an official branch office in Marseille set up by baba just before the war. I will report that I am going there on business and am required to stay for some time. We won't give up this flat. I'll get Raymond to find a flat for us near the Vieux Port and we won't move until everything is clear and aboveboard."

Chapter 19

Conrad

Conrad was eighteen in May 1941. Unlike his siblings, both of whom were fair and blue-eyed, Conrad, nine years older than his younger brother had straight jet-black hair and dark smouldering eyes. This was a little unusual, as both his parents were fair. It was not only the English Harry who was fair, but Olga too was very Armenian and had the usual long face, light brown eyes and a fair complexion. However, his dark looks belied his extraordinarily kind and friendly character – always very patient and gentle with everyone younger than he or whom he felt in any way vulnerable.

He had already received his call-up papers and he duly reported within a week. From the start it was fairly clear that he would be going into the army. It also seemed likely that he would end up as an officer. His fluent knowledge of French and Italian was taken into account by the members of the army Board that interviewed him after his basic training. Of course, this still being public-school dominated England, it was also a major factor that his father was a senior Intelligence Officer with the Royal Navy, and that his grandfather was a retired Colonel.

Within a few more months, Conrad duly arrived in Cairo as a young 2nd Lieutenant in Intelligence. His first posting was to a unit involved in interviewing and screening the many Italian prisoners-of-war gathered in from the collapse of the Italian Abyssinian empire and from the failures of the Italian offensive campaign out of Libya.

Conrad was highly successful in his work. He had a natural talent at putting people at their ease. His dark good looks, black hair and expressive dark eyes gave him a sort of Italian appearance. Most prisoners whom he interviewed assumed that he was in fact Italian, at least in origin. His technique was so good that soon it was he who was interviewing the more senior officers and it was noticeable that he seemed to be able to get more information out of them than anyone else. In the last resort it was a matter of his being 'simpatico' himself. Above all it was sensed by those he interviewed that, unlike his colleagues, he basically liked Italians.

The British attitude towards the Italians at this stage of the war was unique. Deliberate propaganda had created the myth of the 'cowardly' Italian totally unable to stand up to 'our boys'. This created a sort of amused contempt amongst the British officers and also the rank and file. It suited the government to decry the Italian war effort as a counterpart to the continued successes of the Wehrmacht. It was good for civilian morale that at least one of the enemies could be seen as weak. At the same time the diplomats of the foreign office in London, led by Anthony Eden

– Churchill's foreign minister - nourished an irrational and violent hatred of the Italians.

In May 1943 the North African campaign finally came to an end. The German and Italian armies bottled up in Tunis surrendered. The issue for the Western Allies then was where to go from there. The obvious answer for both Churchill and Eden was to strike at Italy itself. An attack on Italy could knock that country out of the war. For Churchill there was the shadow of Gallipoli looming over the whole question. Could he now succeed 25 years later where he had so signally failed in the Great War. The Americans were not so sure. To them Mussolini was a comic opera buffoon and they had none of the angry obsession about the Italians that was common currency among Whitehall bureaucrats. The arguments waged back and forth but eventually one thing became clear and that was that the Allies were not yet ready to invade France and would not be so for some months. Churchill then wrote to Roosevelt saying – "We cannot merely sit and stand idle while enormous numbers of Russians fight in a morass of daily bloodshed." This decided it, and the decision to invade Italy was made. The first landing, within air cover from Tunisia and Malta, was to be in Sicily.

Conrad, still interviewing in Tunis, did not go in with that first wave of invasion forces. The Americans landed at Gela on a perfectly idyllic Mediterranean beach, where only a few hours before they arrived scantily clad girls had been sunning themselves. The British, led by the 5th Division, landed in and around the port of Syracuse. Within days it had fallen and on the 15th July, Conrad together with other follow-up elements, landed in the harbour which had scarcely been damaged at all. Once again Conrad was employed screening Italian prisoners and sifting out as much valuable information as he could ascertain. Soon the Axis hold on the island was limited to a small area at the north-eastern tip round the port of Messina; but meanwhile both the British and Americans had been bogged down in fighting around the slopes of Mount Etna.

Then on the 25th July came the news of dramatic events that had occurred in Rome. A meeting of the Fascist Grand Council had been held that day. Normally Mussolini totally dominated and directed these meetings, which in any case were only rarely held. But on this occasion, as the news from Sicily was being discussed, he failed to do so. Count Grandi, one of the old guard of Fascist leaders who had been with Mussolini from the start, tabled a motion calling on him to 'return' to the King the powers he had taken and which he had so signally failed to implement as far as the armed forces were concerned. It was a vaguely-worded motion which did not seem to amount to much. But to Mussolini's surprise he was outvoted by 19 votes to 7. Even his son-in-law, Count Ciano, had voted in favour of Grandi's motion.

It was only a motion in a fairly powerless assembly, with no formal place in the Italian Constitution and in no way constituted any sort of coup. The next day Mussolini went about his duties, taking no notice whatsoever of the previous night's vote, despite the fact that his wife urged him to have them all arrested and shot. But on that afternoon – the 26th July – a coup did indeed take place and to everyone's surprise it was carried out by the King.

King Victor Emmanuel had, somewhat supinely, acquiesced in Mussolini's assumption of dictatorial powers for the last twenty years without raising a murmur. He was proud of the fact that he was and remained throughout a constitutional monarch. But from his point of view, as the Allies moved forward in Sicily, and as it became clearer to everyone with any perception that the Germans were going to lose the war, something had to be done. He had already been told of what had transpired at the Grand Council and that Count Grandi's motion, calling for Mussolini to hand back his powers to the King, had been passed by a substantial majority. He decided to take the chance that the vote had given him.

When Mussolini arrived for his usual afternoon conference, the King coolly told him that in the circumstances it was his constitutional duty to remove him from office and that he would be appointing a new Prime Minister. The two men then shook hands. What was in Mussolini's thoughts? What made him give up so easily? In the event he left the Palace without another word. Perhaps he believed that he could retrieve the situation with his own loyal supporters. However, once outside the Palace, but still within the grounds, he was arrested by a Captain of the Carabinieri. This officer had already been carefully prepared. Mussolini was told by him that on the King's orders he was being taken into protective custody for his own safety. An ambulance waiting outside the palace whisked him off at speed. That very same evening the King himself broadcast the news on the radio that Mussolini had been dismissed. He calmly informed the Italian public that Marshal Badoglio had been summoned to form a new government.

Almost immediately Badoglio covered himself against any immediate German reaction by stating that the alliance with Germany still held and that the war would continue. No one, neither German nor Italian, really believed him. As it happened, the new Foreign Minister – Guariglia – initiated contacts with the British Legation to the Vatican within three days of the formation of the new government. Feelers were also put out to British diplomatic officials in Lisbon and Madrid. The Germans never knew exactly what was going on, but neither Hitler nor his commander in Italy, Kesselring, were under any illusions. They were well aware that the new government was seeking to find a way out of the war.

Thus began one of the most confused and confusing periods in modern Italian history, when anything – literally anything - could have happened.

Chapter 20

Vichy France – Paris

Meanwhile in Vichy France the occupation was beginning to
bear down more and more heavily on the population. As the Germans took more and more resources and agricultural products out of the country, the shortages of food and fuel bit deep into the morale of the ordinary citizen. People had to queue for everything – not just for the food but for the ration cards to purchase it, for the papers needed to travel anywhere, for the right it would seem to breathe. These paper requirements were all administered by French Vichy officials and they came to be hated. In fact hatred between one French man – or more usually one French woman – and another became widespread throughout the Vichy system.

What Vahan and Nerissa came to fear most as the anti-semitic frenzy got worse was 'denunciation'. Vahan had still not got hold of an Ausweis when he reported the latest information to Nerissa –

"Jean Pierre told me yesterday that these letters of denunciation are pouring in to the Paris Kommandantur at the rate of over 1,000 a day, and the Jews are the foremost target."

"No Vahan, that's ridiculous surely."

"It seems that they all start something like – 'It

is not for me to expose others but I am taking the liberty to…' or 'I would respectfully address you as to the situation at…' and so on and so forth. They do tend to throw many of these away, particularly those unsigned or without an address. But rather than throwing one of these away Jean Pierre kept one which he showed me. It was incredible. I remember the first sentence vividly. It went –

'I have the honour to draw your attention for whatever useful purposes it may serve, that an apartment at 57bis Boulevard Rochechouart, belonging to the Jew Gresalmer contains many fine furniture and silver, valuable paintings and…'

"Oh Vahan no, that's awful, really awful – what have we come to."

"You see my darling, anything can happen, we really have to get out before someone denounces Hakim."

"Well, hokis, get on with it. I've already agreed with you despite my misgivings. It's getting impossible here. This awful business of the yellow star – at least in the south Vichy has stood up against that. I was walking in the middle of the street near the Republique - you know there was no traffic at all and the street was full of pedestrians. I saw this shabby old man coming towards me. He was walking slowly with a stick to help. He was wearing a suit, very frayed and well past its prime. His face was lined but he was sporting a large white moustache rather like Clemenceau's. He had a First World War medal on his lapel. I wouldn't have given him a second look, but then I saw that Yellow Star with 'JUIF' printed across it on his left chest pocket. It was the first time I had seen it. I stopped in my tracks and stood there in the middle of the street as he slowly passed me. In all my life, Vahan, in all my life I have never felt so deeply humiliated. . He never looked at me as he shuffled past staring straight ahead. It was not just shame I felt, Vahan, it was humiliation – not his humiliation, mine!"

As the food situation worsened and the rations were steadily reduced a spirit of 'cocking a snook at the authorities' began to emerge. The women of Paris went to the most extraordinary lengths to maintain their reputation for being chic. When the leather shortage meant that they had to wear wooden clogs, they somehow had them made thicker and higher turning them into a fashion statement. When the failure of electricity made it impossible for them to have their hair permed, they devised more and more elaborate headgears with extravagant flowers to cover themselves. In a quiet way it represented a sort of defiance over the conquering male domination. The only young men in the streets were of course German.

In a similar spirit the young boys in the streets made their own fashion statement. Their fathers of course were all either prisoners of war, still two million of them, or had been gathered up for forced labour in the Reich, or were in hiding. The kids became what were known as 'zazous'. They wore their hair long greased with oil, they sported long jackets, high collars and drainpipe trousers. They affected dark glasses, chunky unpolished shoes or clogs and, unaccountably, furled-up umbrellas which they never opened even when it was pouring with rain. They listened to jazz played loudly, knowing that the Germans and Vichy officials frowned on it as the product of negro and despised American culture.

As the Asadourian family waited for the necessary papers to come through to enable them to move to the unoccupied zone, Vahan spent a lot of his time in the streets. On one occasion he returned home in a particularly depressed mood and sounded off to Nerissa and Hakim at the dinner table. His sense of humour was notoriously rather poor and living with the perpetually serious-minded Nerissa had not helped. He grumbled –

"How can they be so frivolous? Haven't they noticed the disgraceful collapse of their country. They seem to be totally disinterested."

"What are you talking about? People are so preoccupied in queuing in one place or another for food or for other basics, they simply haven't the time to think of concepts like 'the nation'."

"No, no. I am talking about those young lads – what are they called – zazous. I see them every day in the Metro. You can hear them talking about food or jazz or the latest record, boys and girls fourteen or even older, laughing, cuddling, openly kissing and 'tutoying' everybody in sight. You see them queuing for the cinema and going from one cinema to the next."

"Oh Vahan, come on, it sounds like the age-old complaint of one generation about the next one down – it's been like that for centuries."

"No, no this is different. For them nothing is happening and they are too stupid and yes igno-rant to take any interest in the political…"

"Baba," said Hakim – they were of course talk-ing together in Armenian as usual when no stran-gers were present, "I do think that that's unfair."

"Why?" snapped Vahan.

He realised that he was finding himself irrita-ble a lot of the time but he couldn't help himself and he didn't know why. Malnutrition has a sub-tle psychological effect over and above the purely physical one. It makes people tired and irritable without them realising it. Money was beginning to mean less and less. Nerissa did her best, but scrounging, sucking up to shopkeepers, finding the best value on the black market, and all those little stratagems employed by almost the whole native French female population, was not within Nerissa's capacity. As a result the Asadourians' diet probably was worse than less affluent fami-lies.

"Go on Hakim – come out with your opinion – don't mind your father," said Nerissa, glaring at Vahan, who had the grace to acknowledge that he was in the wrong and turned to listen to what his son had to say.

"Well, what I mean is that they can't make any overt political statement, can they? They're only kids – you said 14 or 15, But there are some – actually quite a few – in my school who try to act as zazous and they are only 12 or 13. They are far too young to go off and join the 'Resistants', and too young to come out with any political opinions, which would be dangerous in any case. What they are doing is to thumb their noses at the adult world – and remember, baba, that for them the adult world is not their own fathers, but the Germans."

Vahan smiled at his son with real pleasure and said –

"Good heavens you're quite right Hakim. I didn't see it that way – though I still think that most of them aren't acting consciously like you say. But you are right – if only one or two are aware of what they are doing, then they are absolved."

"There are even a couple of the boys in my class – both trying to be zazous like their older brothers - who have taken to wearing yellow stars themselves. It made me feel so bad. Most of the boys know that I have a Jewish background and yet I don't wear the yellow star because you have forbidden me to do so – while they have donned it ostentatiously as a badge of pride".

"My dear Hakim the reasoning behind both decisions is totally different. For you it separates you, completely unjustifiably, from the rest of society; for them it is part of a general desire to shock the adult world. They are not making an anti-Vichy statement. I suspect that the puritanical Resistance finds them just as objectionable as does Vichy. They are simply mocking adult politics."

"But baba it is not entirely without danger for them – they are often beaten up in the streets by those short-haired, youth-movement Petainist louts."

"Oh dear. It is all so complicated. Anyway, one thing one can say is that it's certainly not collaboration of any kind. They ignore the Germans probably only because they are not interested, but actually, ignoring them is the best way of dealing with the dilemma we all face."

"But Vahan," said Nerissa, this whole matter of not seeing them, not acknowledging their presence, can sometimes be tricky,"

"Certainly – but to withhold speech is in a way to refuse collaboration."

"Yes, but somehow it all so often turns out wrong. I was walking across the Place du Chatelet the other day. There was this German soldier, honestly Vahan he couldn't have been more than 18 years old. He was clearly lost and looking perplexed. He came up to me and asked for directions to the Notre-Dame. I didn't speak to him, like you have always advised; but instead I pointed up, perhaps I admit a little contemptuously, at the twin towers rising up to the sky on the other side of the river – a child could have seen them. He blushed bright red, mumbled something and walked off towards the river. On one level I felt satisfied that he clearly felt himself

to be a fool. Then I became ashamed of my petti-
ness and thought to myself – my God what have
we come to."

"It's not easy – it's not easy and it's getting
more dangerous all the time. We have to leave
Paris and go to the unoccupied zone as soon as
we can."

Chapter 21

Rome

It was the 1st August 1943, a week after the fall of Mussolini, when Conrad was summoned to a meeting called by General Maxwell Taylor, a senior commander of the elite US 82nd Airborne Division. Conrad was still stationed in Syracuse, but he was being driven all round the Allied section of Sicily in a jeep that had been put at his disposal. He was being required, over and over again, to act as an interpreter between American and British officers appointed as local governors and those civilian local officials and mayors whose collaboration was desired. This collaboration was being given freely without any complexes or reservations, but interpretation was often needed. The meeting to which Conrad had been called was to take place in Palermo. It was to be held in the medieval royal palace which was now General Patton's headquarters.

That morning Conrad was in Enna. He was driven at top speed in his jeep through the countryside and into Palermo. Once at the palace he was led up a winding narrow staircase at the rear of the building. He was told to wait on a bench outside a door behind which the murmur of some sort of conference could be heard. He waited over an hour and then was called in. Inside, he stood firmly at attention in front of the men on the other side of a large oval table. His own commanding officer was there to one side. He recognised the American General Maxwell Taylor seated in the middle. There were also three other military officers, two Americans and one British whom he knew to be a senior officer in Military Intelligence. General Taylor did all the talking –

"Ah, Lieutenant Bridgeman – stand at ease – at ease. George pull up a chair for the young man."

Conrad removed his cap and sat down on the chair brought up for him – but he remained at attention as five pairs of rather steely eyes stared hard at him..

"You are no doubt aware of the news that Mussolini has fallen from power"

"Yes sir, certainly."

"Would you be at all surprised then to be told that the new government of Marshal Badoglio has been putting out feelers towards a possible separate peace. By the way I am sure that you appreciate that everything said in this room is highly classified and that...."

"I can assure you sir," Conrad's own commanding officer interrupted, "that Lieutenant Bridgeman is well aware of the importance of secrecy in these matters."

Conrad said nothing.

"Well Lieutenant, you haven't replied to my first question."

"Oh, sorry sir. No! I wouldn't be the slightest bit surprised. No one, certainly no Italian that I have interviewed, has believed for a minute his assurances that the war would continue. On the contrary I would have been surprised if there had been no such feelers."

"Good – good. Well the fact of the matter is that George and I are proposing to go and meet Badoglio and the commander of the Rome garrison in Rome itself soon, if it can be arranged. The position is enormously complicated. The first question facing us is what is to become of the Italian army if we can get round to agreeing some sort of armistice? Then there is bound to be an immediate and violent German reaction. Just as you didn't believe Badoglio's assertion that the war would continue – neither will Hitler. In any case they are not just going to let all that industrial power in the Po valley just vanish. So in view of all this, the issue is whether there is any way we can cooperate with the Italians."

Conrad was only twenty but here he was at the very centre of an important and complex political discussion. He was very excited, but he still had no idea why he had been called to this meeting. The sheer thrill of finding himself on the fringe listening to what was clearly an important military conference kept him on the edge of his seat. There was a short pause as an aide – a full Major nevertheless – entered and handed a note to the General.

"Ah yes. Bridgeman, I'm afraid I have to cut this meeting a bit short. I'll get right to the point. The fact is that before George and I can go, we really need someone to get into Rome and prepare the necessary ground for setting up a meeting. Your CO has recommended you. I am told that all the Italians you interview, and you have now interviewed hundreds, all take you to be a native-born Italian. You are already trained in all the necessary techniques of wireless communication. However this is technically behind enemy lines and you will not be in uniform, accordingly it must be completely voluntary."

Conrad looked at his CO who nodded at him, confirming that he had already thrashed all this out with the American General. Conrad then turned to the General and said without thinking much about it and without any sort of heroics –

"I will be happy to do the job sir."

"Good! Good! You will be fully briefed by your CO who is in charge of the operation at this end. I should add that as yet no armistice has been agreed never mind signed. Anything at all could yet happen and we might never actually make the trip. But for the moment our political masters are of the opinion that in the event of an armistice being agreed, the American 82nd Airborne division could parachute directly into Rome. This would enable us to take the city and help the Italians defend it in the event of a violent German response. In any case, even if none of this turns out as we are planning, it would still be advantageous to have an efficient Intelligence agent inside the city whatever happens."

During the next few days Conrad was kept very busy. He was provided with the radio set that he was to use. He was given the names and addresses of those who were to be his contacts when he arrived in Rome. They included a Polish officer, who had been there under cover for nearly a year, and three Italian Communists, residents of the city, initially recruited by the Pole. For two weeks Conrad was intensively briefed daily on all aspects of his mission. Plans of the city layout showing where he was going to live had to be studied, papers had to be prepared and he had to learn exactly who he was and where he came from. Finally he was told that he would be given the rank of acting Captain to give him some extra authority when dealing with people in Rome.

At last the day came when he boarded the small British submarine which was going to take him to the rendezvous just off the Italian coast north of Ostia. It was the 19th August and Messina had at last fallen. Sicily was now under the full control of the Allies. The German troops and even most of the Italians that had been defending the town had been successfully evacuated onto the mainland and the attacking allies had been unable to prevent it. Conrad in a state of immense exhilaration chatted with the young men on the submarine. He was not without fear, but it was a fear that excited him, not one that paralysed. The rendezvous, timed for the hour before midnight, went without a hitch. When the submarine surfaced, the fishing boat that was meeting them was already there, bobbing about on the dark waters. The whole thing passed in a whirl of activity. One moment he was shaking hands with two strangers, the next the old van in which they travelled had already stopped in front of a dilapidated house in the Tiburtina district of the Eternal City, where he was due to live.

Conrad never knew, and he never would, that his biological father had made the same journey on a very similar mission behind enemy lines. In that case it was into Smyrna, behind Greek lines, twenty years earlier. What he did know, however, was the thrill that he felt in the absolute and certain knowledge that his own father, his only father, the father who had loved and nurtured him all his life, would be proud of him if he knew what he was doing.

Rome, always so conscious of its great and glorious past, by 1943 was run down and shabby. Protected by the presence in its midst of the Vatican City, it had not as yet been bombed once. But food was in short supply and the ordinary everyday services on which any city relies, such as transport, electricity supply, or the telephone service, were not functioning well. The population was listless and confused. The outburst of joy in the streets when the King announced the fall of Mussolini and the appointment of a new government was shortlived. Everyone feared for the future and all were aware that sooner or later a violent German reaction was inevitable.

Conrad had set up his radio in the attic of the house in which he was staying. The owner, one of the men who had met him on the coast when Conrad had come ashore, was a dedicated Communist, a member of the PCI, the only political party which had any real organisation at this stage. Conrad had to be very careful; any healthy young man on the streets not in uniform was immediately very conspicuous. Giancarlo, his Communist host, found an Italian army uniform for him, but even that was dangerous. In the end Conrad fashioned himself some bandages and an arm sling. He also put on a gauze eye patch over his left eye. Thus it was that he was able to move about the city. His forged papers were well made and never gave any trouble, though he was often stopped in the street and asked to show them.

The situation after the fall of Mussolini was so confusing that most ordinary Italian citizens were quite unable to unravel what was happening to them. In the north of the country their former allies – the Germans – were slowly infiltrating more and more elite divisions into the country. There was nothing secret about this. The Commando Supremo of Italy would be officially informed that another crack division would be moving down the Brenner Pass into Italy to help in the fight against the threatened Anglo-American invasion in the south. The new government tried to limit these movements but could not openly object – the two countries were supposed to be allied and all the Germans were doing was coming to help.

Meanwhile in Rome, the government began

abolishing all the Fascist paraphernalia of the previous regime, and that aspect of the coup was going well. But the Italians were slow in fixing up talks with the Anglo-Americans for an armistice. Both the King and Badoglio and his ministers desperately wanted to end the war as soon as possible, as indeed did most of the population. But the government was caught in a vice. Their hope was that Italy could at a stroke become neutral; that the Germans in the north would quietly leave and retire north of the Alps; that the Anglo-Americans would also give up and perhaps even retire back to North Africa. It was pure wishful thinking on their part. There was simply no way at all, no manner of argument or action which could have resulted in such an outcome. It suited neither the Germans nor the Anglo-Americans – but nevertheless the chimera of neutrality always hovered over the Italian leaders.

One of the problems facing Badoglio and the King was that many of the best units of the Italian army were outside Italy. Really the only sensible course would have been for the government to have done everything in its power during these weeks to bring as many of those units currently in the East, in Yugoslavia, in Greece and in the Greek islands, back to mainland Italy. What they needed was a functioning army as a bargaining counter, perhaps situated in and around Rome, capable of being thrown into the scales for one side or the other. But in the end they did absolutely nothing. There was a complete lack of leadership at all levels, from the King and Badoglio at the top down to the junior officers of the regular army at the bottom.

Mussolini was dismissed on the 26th July but serious discussions between the Royal government and the Western allies did not begin until the 19th August, a few days after the fall of Messina and the day that Conrad himself arrived in Rome. Conrad's radio voice was not the only information going out from Rome to the Allied commanders – but it became one of the ones to which they listened most carefully.

The substantive negotiations took place in Lisbon between one of Eisenhower's most trusted aides – General Bedell Smith – and a senior Italian general – General Castellano. If both before and during these negotiations some part of the Italian army could have been returned to Italy, and then within Italy organised and prepared for a German attack, Italy might have been spared the terrible events that followed. However, so anxious was the King and the government that everything should be kept secret to avoid provoking the Germans, that no preparations were made. Scarcely a single important Italian officer, currently in command of troops, was informed of what was afoot. It was a ridiculous policy as Hitler and the German High Command had long since surmised that negotiations were going on. The Germans were quietly preparing to take over in the north immediately Italy became neutral or changed sides, and were stationing troops close to Italian forces both in the centre and the south ready to disarm them the moment the order was given.

On the 3rd September the two negotiators finally signed an armistice. The urgent question remaining was when and how it would be announced, and until it was so announced how was the Italian government to act. The Italians wanted an invasion to be mounted before the Armistice was announced. The Western allies, anxious not to be opposed in the proposed landing by any Italian forces, wanted the Armistice to be announced first. It would also have the effect, so they thought, of disrupting any opposition before they landed. In the end the real issue was Rome. Who would get there first? When the armistice had been signed, Castellano and Bedell Smith, the two negotiators, had considered that when the armistice was announced, the US 82nd Airborne division would take Rome. Once installed there the division would help the Italian army to defend the city and keep the Germans at bay. The invasion would then take place halfway up the Italian peninsula and those German forces in the south would be caught in a trap.

But what was the situation on the ground in Rome? The Allied commanders decided that a senior officer from the 82nd Airborne had to go personally and find out. Conrad had been asked to report on which Italian units were in or near the city. He had duly radioed what he had been able to find out. He had also warned that morale was not good and that the confusion in the minds of all the Italian civilians in the city was mirrored as far as he could see in the military. Above all, he had had no contact with any of the Italian leaders. In the end it was decided, as originally envisaged, that General Maxwell Taylor should go to Rome with an aide to confer with Badoglio and General Carboni, currently in command of the Rome garrison.

Conrad was ordered to liaise with a senior officer on Badoglio's staff – an army man not a civilian bureaucrat. It was not too difficult making all the necessary arrangements for the meeting and there was no danger – there were no German soldiers in Rome. Accordingly, on the agreed day, an official car containing Conrad and an Italian Colonel, followed by a second car with three armed guards, arrived in the early evening at a rendezvous on a beach just north of Ostia. Conrad himself was in civilian clothes, but he had not bothered on this occasion with his eye-patch or his arm sling. . Unknown to the Italian Colonel in the first car Conrad had also organised, with the help of Giancarlo, for a large third black car to follow them discreetly. This had been crammed with five PCI enthusiasts all heavily armed. In the event, it was not needed, but treachery was in the air throughout these days and Conrad sensed it all around him.

"Ah Captain Bridgeman – we meet again," was Maxwell Taylor's first comment as he jumped out of the launch and shook hands. Conrad felt a boyish thrill at being addressed as Captain by someone for the first time. He introduced the Italian Colonel to the general and his aide and explained the plan for the rest of the day. Then with Conrad and the two Americans in the first car and the Italian Colonel now in the second, they drove off back to Rome. In the car, General Taylor put Conrad into the picture.

"Clearly, Captain, we don't want to slug it out, fighting our way up the Italian peninsula, if we can help it. The best way to avoid that would be to take and hold Rome by a coup de main. The main landing would still have to be further south near Naples. But so long as we can have clear and useful support from the Italian army, we could take Rome with a parachute drop – perhaps landing a supporting infantry division in one of the ports nearby as well."

"That sounds fine, sir", said Conrad. "I guarantee that you will be welcomed with open arms by the great majority of the population here. I know – I've seen and talked to many over the past few weeks. But, sir, you will have to be careful about the help you hope to get from the Italian army units stationed here in Rome. Morale is low and they are not well equipped. Furthermore there are still some units among them that are pro-fascist."

"Can they operate as a disciplined army?"

"That I can't say, sir. I have only talked to the occasional soldier. The soldiers themselves will fight if they are properly led and have equipment, but…"

"Ah well – we'll have to see."

There was then a short silence as the Americans pondered. Then the General turned to Conrad and said –

"By the way, Captain, I have noticed for some time that the second car is being followed some way back by another large car that seems to contain…"

"Not to worry sir, they are my men. The situation here in Rome is confused. There is treachery everywhere and I thought that a bit of back-up firepower might be useful. Mind you, sir, I don't anticipate any real trouble".

"OK, fine. Listen Bridgeman you better come in with us for the conference just in case there is any need for interpretation. I believe that Badoglio understands English well, but I don't know about Carboni. Anyway no harm, though I don't want your cover compromised."

"No that's fine they won't take any notice of me."

The two cars entered Rome and eventually swung into the courtyard of the Palazzo Caprara, where the Americans were to meet Badoglio and General Carboni.

For three hours the Italian Head of State – that is what he chose to call himself mimicking Mussolini – and General Carboni talked with Taylor. Time and again the Americans pressed Badoglio as to the fighting capacity of the Rome Garrison and time and again Badoglio prevaricated. The fact was that for the month or more that Badoglio and the King had been in power, they had done nothing – nothing at all – to see to the morale of the garrison or their capacity to defend their own capital. The two sides were at total cross purposes. The Italians wanted the Allies to take on the task of fighting the Germans on their own, while the Allies felt they could not do so with a mere parachute jump without having Italian military help.

It was 2.00 a.m. when the two Americans and Conrad finally walked down to where a Red Cross ambulance was waiting for them in the courtyard.

"Good God – what's this Captain?" said the American general.

"Sir we had a problem. Cars, even official ones, would be very conspicuous driving through the empty town after the midnight curfew. This is really the safest solution in the circumstances. I do have the same back-up as before but they will be behind us."

"Very well, Captain. Are you coming with us?"

"Certainly sir – I will return with the back-up after you have gone."

All three then clambered into the back of the van and settled on the two beds at each side. There was a long silence as the ambulance swung out of the Palazzo Caprara and began the drive to the coast. Eventually Maxwell Taylor turned to his aide and said wearily –

"It's impossible, Gardiner, we couldn't possibly take the risk. I have all the lives of those young men to think about. The Italians could not suggest anything concrete – not a rendezvous – not a plan – not anything.

"But sir, however efficient the Germans may be, it must take them at least two days before they could react and get to the outskirts of the city – never mind entering it. Surely, even if the Italians couldn't hold up the Germans for more than a day or two, it would give us enough time to bring in an Infantry division at a nearby port and prepare defences."

"No! Look, the reason for a drop would be to hold the capital for at least a couple of weeks – not to start a street-by-street fight for it. What do you say Captain, you were there and heard everything. What about the muttered asides in Italian between them?"

"No sir, there was little there that wasn't open – I think they suspected that I understood Italian. But I do agree with you sir. It seems clear that they want to take Italy out of the war but without having to do any more fighting. They were clearly disappointed that you seemed to indicate that the main invasion would be coming in the south. Ideally what they want is for us to fight the Germans for them well north of the city."

"But then are you saying that you think that a drop on the city would be too risky."

"Oh no sir, I wouldn't presume…er…I do agree with Colonel Gardiner that the Germans must take a minimum of two or three days to arrive, and it would be an enormous gain if we could take and hold the city intact until the main forces arrive."

"But look here, the Germans are both north and south of us. We could be caught like rats in a trap."

"But sir," said Gardiner. "If you are suggesting that the Germans in the south who would be facing an invasion would come rushing north to trap us, then that would mean that our invasion would be virtually unopposed and our forces would come racing up after them."

"Maybe, maybe – but the 82nd and all those young lives would be goners."

When they reached the coast, the launch was already waiting to take them back to the submarine lying somewhere in the distance offshore. Everyone shook hands and Conrad stood waiting in the dark as the launch departed. He slowly walked back up the sand dunes to the road. The ambulance had already gone. He stood for what seemed to be a long time, no longer able to see the water in the dark but hearing the lap of the waves. At last the car filled with the rough PCI men, most no older than he and all by now very drunk including the driver, arrived and they were on their way back to Rome as dawn broke.

There was never any airdrop into Rome. Instead, it took nine more months of desperate and bloody fighting before the next uniformed Allied soldier would arrive in the city. During those nine months Conrad remained in Rome sending his weekly reports from the attic of the house in the Tiburtina.

Chapter 22

Nicolai and Sima

The eldest of the Avakian sisters – Sima – had married a penniless Russian aristocrat – Count Nicolai Androv. This young man had arrived in Constantinople early in 1920 a refugee from the Crimea. He had been a junior officer in General Wrangel's White army which had been operating in the south of Russia during the last stages of the Russian Civil War. Part of the defeated White army, he had arrived in Sevastopol with the rest of the fleeing army just ahead of the pursuing Reds. There, meeting up with his mother, the Countess Natalie Androvna, and his young brother, he managed to get himself and his family onto the huge fleet of large and small vessels which constituted the fairly orderly evacuation fleet. These ships arrived in Constantinople, then under British occupation, and disgorged its large number of Russian refugees – almost 150,000 people. It was ironic that after 300 years of failed Russian attempts to take the great city, Constantinople temporarily had more Russians in it than ever before or ever since.

Sima Avakian had fallen in love with the young Nicolai most unsuitably. Her father Karekin had not objected and they had married. Nicolai had been offered a post in Karekin's business, but he had turned it down. Instead, after sending his mother to visit her sister in Italy, who was married to an Italian Count – the Conte Maggi – he and Sima had joined her there. The Conte Maggi had extensive estates in the Veneto and needed help in managing them. Nicolai went to work for him and he and Sima had been in Italy ever since.

At the same time as Vahan and Nerissa were contemplating moving to the unoccupied zone of Vichy France, and Conrad was living in Rome sending his weekly reports back, Nicolai and Sima's position in Italy was becoming more difficult. Nicolai had so far kept carefully out of Italian politics during his time in the country. However it was inevitable that his employer – the Conte Maggi – should be associated throughout the thirties with the local Fascists. He was not interested in the theories behind the Fascist movement, but as the local landed aristocrat, he appreciated the calm and order which Mussolini appeared to have brought to Italy. He did not believe, as did some, that this was the calm and order of the grave. Maggi was a good Catholic and the Mussolini Concordat with the Church confirmed for him that Mussolini was a leader worth supporting. Whether he would have continued that support once war broke out and Mussolini took the fatal decision to join in, was not so clear. He had died in 1939 as the result of a fall from his horse when out hunting, so his views on that question would never be known.

Nicolai had been a stateless refugee without Italian citizenship until Maggi had finally managed to get naturalisation papers for him, though the final papers did not come through until after the old Count had died. Nicolai had accordingly kept a very low profile on the politics of the state. The local peasants and tenant farmers had come to trust and like him. He was an efficient overseer of the Count's estates. He was fair, even if a bit cool and humourless, in his dealings with them. When it came down to it, however, the local farmers preferred efficiency to charm. They thought of him as a good man but not really very 'simpatico'. Both the tenant peasants and the local Veneto fascists simply assumed that he was a natural supporter of the regime, somewhat like the great majority of the Italian people – without thinking about it much.

Although Nicolai was 40 when the Italians joined in the Second World War, he had not been required to join the army. He was technically still a foreigner with his old Nansen passport, until his naturalisation papers were finalised. Then even after the papers came through, as a food producing manager of a large estate, he was exempt from call-up. But it was the war which finally brought him face to face with the political problems of his adopted country for the first time. The alliance with Hitler's Germany and the degrading Declaration of War on France, already defeated by the Germans, sickened him and he began questioning the whole basis of Mussolini's foreign policy. From there it was only a short step to start questioning the whole foundation of the

Fascist state.

Nicolai and Sima were very self-sufficient and did not have many Italian friends. But one of these friends was another Count who came from Florence and had property there and lands in the Po valley. Nicolai and he were of a similar age. They had met at a reception in Florence given at the Poggio Imperiale, a rather superior school in the city, renowned for its Fascist sympathies. This new friend – Count Pietro Bellini – was like the late Conte Maggi a mild supporter of the regime – in his case largely due to his deeply-held anti-communist views.

The arrest and imprisonment of Mussolini and the surrender of Italy that followed shortly afterwards, thrust the whole nature of the Italian state and its future course into the forefront of everybody's mind, and this included Nicolai. During these months Nicolai and Sima were again in Florence staying with Nicolai's mother – the Countess Natalya Androvna - in her apartment in the Palazzo Maggi. A few weeks after the fall of Mussolini came the news of the armistice negotiated by Badoglio and the unconditional surrender. German reaction was, as expected, swift, highly efficient and ruthless. Italian forces were everywhere disarmed and there were many instances of assassination of officers who did not supinely comply with German orders. The already confused situation became a complete morass of uncertainty. Civil War did not immediately break out, but the army completely disintegrated. Some of the army units refused to surrender to the Allies and went over to the Germans; other units simply melted away; whilst some waited in disarray for orders from the Royal government.

The Western Allies had sent an American general to confer secretly with the Italians in Rome over a possible airdrop of American paratroopers to help the Italian army defend the city. However, the Italians had failed to make any watertight military arrangements. The whole affair was a complete mess and Eisenhower refused to delay the armistice or the invasion when requested to do so by the King's government. The Italian leadership, such as it was, managed both to alienate its ally-turned-enemy, who continued to disarm and neutralise any Italian units it could lay its hands on, while at the same time alienating its enemy-turned-ally almost as much.

But it got worse. Eisenhower's broadcast announcement of the signing of the armistice was read over the BBC on the 8th September, despite every effort that was made by the Badoglio government to have it delayed. Conrad and his PCI toughs listened to the announcement as it came over the airwaves, with Conrad translating breathlessly as his comrades became more and more excited. He was out on the streets immediately, ready to report back on the reactions of the people of Rome. As he had assured General Taylor, the population was overjoyed. They all thought that this meant that the war was over for them. Little did they realise that, on the contrary, for most Italians it was just about to begin in earnest.

As the news of the armistice spread, the King himself and the senior Generals realised that their total failure of leadership had created a complete catastrophe. Badoglio himself went onto the radio within hours confirming the armistice and ordering all Italian forces to cease hostilities against Anglo-American soldiers. But the broadcast did not make the situation clear as to whether the German forces should be opposed or not. While his broadcast confirmed the joy of the civilians, it left an enormous vacuum for what remained of the Italian army. Then, not more than a few hours later, came the final and complete political collapse of the Italian state apparatus. The King panicked. In the middle of that night of the 8th/9th September he gathered up his personal belongings and with all his family he drove out of Rome in a small fleet of black motorcars.

Although roving about in the streets Conrad did not see the Royal family go. Carefully listening to all the excited buzz of conversation about the two broadcasts in the streets, he eventually found himself near the Palazzo Caprara. It was then that he saw a motorcade of cars driving out with Badoglio's own car in the lead, clearly heading out of Rome. Conrad grasped immediately what this meant. During the course of the rest of the evening he saw various other cars containing senior Generals and their families, who, getting wind of what was happening, were themselves also abandoning the capital. Once he realised the full extent of the exodus he hurried home to report on the situation.

It was a clear and blatant abandonment of a people still celebrating and imagining that they were about to enter a period of peace. Conrad's PCI bodyguard who were with him were all for firing at the last of the cars as they drove off. But Conrad, anxious to get back and make his report, managed to persuade them not to engage in anything rash and unplanned. Several of Conrad's PCI comrades did however join the all-party Committee of National Liberation, which was formed about two days later, and which began its political life by roundly condemning Victor Emmanuel and Badoglio for their complete failure of leadership and precipitate abandonment of the capital and its people.

The King and Badoglio did eventually reach the Adriatic coast. There they embarked on two motor launches, each capable of holding only about 150 people. This was not enough for all the Generals and civil officials that had poured out after the King, and some had to return sheepishly to Rome. The two launches arrived in Brindisi just hours after British troops moving up from Sicily entered the town. Indeed they only just managed to evade attack by British patrol boats by frantically waving white flags.

The whole exercise was a disaster. Suddenly German soldiers, German tanks, German trucks filled with troops, were everywhere in every city north of Naples, and particularly in Rome. It would appear that Victor Emmanuel had not surrendered his country to the Western Allies but to the Germans. And what of the remnants of the Italian army? Here too there was a complete collapse of leadership – a collapse that showed that twenty years of Fascism had in the end been a complete and utter failure. Literally hundreds of officers abandoned their men and melted away. This left the men leaderless and unable to stand up to the terrible and ruthless revenge taken by the bitterly angry Germans. Thousands of Italian soldiers all over Yugoslavia and Greece were shot – not only those trying to put up some resistance but also those who surrendered. Those rounded up in Italy were sent as forced labour battalions to the Reich.

Then, within a day or two of the King's panicked flight came the daring rescue of the imprisoned Mussolini. He had been moved around from one prison to another, but had come to rest in a remote hotel at the top of the Gran Sasso mountains in the centre of Italy. He was rescued by a special task force which was sent by Hitler, who was determined to try and save a man whom he had always thought of as a friend. Mussolini, not really that anxious to be freed and forced back into the role of Hitler's auxilliary, was bullied into setting up a rump Fascist state in that part of Italy still not taken by the Allies.

Thus the scene was set for a terrible confrontation throughout Italy with over a year of bitter and bloody fighting up and down the peninsula, with Italians fighting Italians as well as conventional forces. There was a German army fighting an Anglo-American army; regular Italian troops of the Royal army fighting alongside the Western Allies; regular Italian Fascist troops fighting alongside the Germans; Italian partisans under the Committee of Liberation fighting Fascist militia; German SS anti-partisan units fighting against the whole Italian people. Trapped in the middle of it all were hundreds of thousands of ordinary Italian families, betrayed by their former leaders and uncertain of the rough and sometimes brutal Partisans. They could do little except struggle to survive the resulting disease, bombing and starvation.

Chapter 23

Nerissa in revolt

Nerissa was probably eating worse than Vahan and Hakim. If it was just a matter of money to get extra rations, she could afford to pay. But so often getting enough food, over and above the meagre ration, was not just a matter of paying. You had to know how to manipulate the Black Market – how to cajole those little extras from the shopkeeper – how to queue and wheedle and scrounge – how to take the train out into the country and get that something extra. This was second-nature to most French wives and mothers, but was quite beyond Nerissa. Then, what food that was available tended to be piled first on Hakim's plate and then Vahan's.

Most of Nerissa's friends were on the left politically and were almost all highly critical of Vichy and all it stood for. As the weeks went by following the introduction of the Yellow Star, Nerissa became ever more outspoken. Whether malnutrition was making her light-headed, or whether it was just Avakian bloody-mindedness, she suddenly got it into her head to join some of her lefty friends and start wearing the Yellow Star herself. She got hold of one and wrote the word "Ortodoxe" on it. She was well aware that the Armenian church to which she belonged was not an Orthodox church, but thought it would have more resonance, as of course the word also applied to a particular sect of Jews. Vahan was absolutely furious with her and did not mince his words –

"What you are doing, my girl, is drawing attention to yourself and by extension to the family. We already have the problem of Hakim's identity papers that identify him as a Jew. Why are you doing it? What are you trying to say? What would your action accomplish?"

"I don't know. I don't know. I just felt so humiliated seeing that old man shuffling across the street. It is so totally immoral. I just feel I have to make some sort of a stand, make some sort of a gesture. Don't look at me like that – I know, I know, it's not going to make a mite of difference – but by God it helps me live with myself. Look at those kids, those teenage zazous wearing the yellow star. They are regularly reviled by the Vichy press. They are smugly compared with the collaborationist's ideal of a youth movement consisting of cold showers and healthy communal sing-songs – all those short-haired Petainist louts".

"But Nerissa why you?"

This came out almost in a whisper and Nerissa scarcely even heard it – but carried straight on –

"These kids may not be entirely clear what they mean by flouting a Yellow Star – it may well just be cocking a snook at the adult world. But Vahan, it is dangerous for them, even if it is only a game. The German soldiers may do nothing, but they are regularly beaten up in the streets by French louts for showing disrespect."

"Nerissa – it's not our problem."

At this, Nerissa looked hard at Vahan and for once said nothing. There was a silence which stretched out longer than usual, and in fact nothing further was said between them on the matter. Vahan believed he was right. A low-profile in these circumstances was necessary. It had been the same in Ottoman Turkey in the years 1915/16. Survival had depended on looking away. But for the first time – for the first time, as he looked at the wife, whom he adored, he was no longer quite so sure.

The Paris police were faced with a curious situation once the Yellow Star rules were introduced. They were under strict orders to arrest any they knew to be Jews who refused to wear the emblem. But what were they to do with those who they knew were not Jews who chose to wear it. By the beginning of 1943 some of the internment camps had been taken over by the SS – though the largest and meanest – Drancy itself, remained under French administration for many more months. This period also saw the first signs of a loosening of overt police support for the German authorities.

It was in these circumstances, that Nerissa took to going out with her provocative yellow star. She was absolutely amazed to find, despite the virulent anti-semitism of the Press and of most of the French haute bourgeoisie, that she received a lot of open sympathy from her ordinary French neighbours in the streets. On several occasions, when she stood at the edge of the inevitable queue at the bakers or the grocery, she would be motioned to the front (Jews were not allowed to join queues) so that she could be served first and could get away. It proved once and for all to her that French anti-semitism had little strength in the working class – it was very much a movement of the Catholic Right-wing.

Eventually, however, the moment came when she was arrested by a French Gendarme. She had been queuing at the butcher's shop, and was waiting patiently in the middle of the queue, when a policeman walking by grabbed hold of her and took her down to the local police station. The other women in the queue hissed but said nothing as she was led away. At the police station she produced her papers, but she was well known at the station, where she had for years come to register annually, a requirement both for the family visa and as a visiting alien. It was early in the evening and she was placed in one of the cells overnight. A policeman, who knew the family, volunteered to go and warn Vahan.

When he arrived at the apartment, Vahan had not as yet begun to worry, as he knew how long it took to shop for anything, but of course got very agitated when the friendly Gendarme arrived and explained what had happened –

"We have Mdme Asadourian, monsieur, at the station. She has been formally arrested."

Vahan knew at once why she had been arrested, but was determined to seek out on what grounds the police had to imprison her.

"On what charge, officer, has she been arrested."

"Sir – it is a bit difficult, and we are most upset with the man who arrested her. I can only say that he is new at this station and he will be set right. But your wife, sir, who we all know is Armenian was wearing the yellow star, which should only be worn by Jews. Admittedly the word 'Juif' was not written on it, but ...er...well...it is subversive of... er...the occupation rules."

The conversation blundered on and Vahan began to get seriously worried when the officer said that Nerissa would have to remain in custody overnight. The following morning she would be handed over to the Germans. It was now a question of urgency and Vahan spent a long time persuading the officer, who was in fact the senior officer on duty that night, that he would see that the wearing of the yellow star would cease, and that he would come down to the station to collect her. A fairly substantial sum of money changed hands. More to the point Vahan managed to unearth one of the last bottles of brandy left in the apartment and handed it over, to be shared at the station. The officer accepted with a smile, but refused to let Vahan come that evening to collect her. Instead it was arranged that Vahan could come the next morning. He was also put on parole to make sure that there would be no more yellow stars.

That night at the station, once the duty officer

returned from seeing Vahan and the station was closed for the night, Nerissa was taken out of her cell. The brandy bottle was opened and the three policemen manning the station played cards with her. One of the men went out to buy some cheap wine, with some of the money handed over by Vahan, and this augmented the brandy which quickly disappeared. They were all keen bridge players and needed a fourth. Nerissa had always been a good bridge partner, always deferring to her partner, particularly to male partners. She ended up playing as partner with each and, to her own surprise and pleasure, charming all three. More money was spent on food, the station store was raided for cheese and biscuits and the men shared their substantial meal with her. Ironically Nerissa ate better that night under arrest than she had done for many weeks.

The next morning Vahan arrived early, but could not get in and had to wait outside until the front door was opened for business. Nerissa, looking a bit sheepish and without the yellow star which had been torn off her coat the night before – came out. Vahan and Nerissa rarely embraced in public, but Vahan's sense of relief as he saw Nerissa emerge from the police station overcame his usual reserve in these matters, and he clasped her tight, there and then, in the middle of the street.

When they got home, Hakim had already left for school. Vahan made it clear that he had given his promise that she would not under any circumstances go out again wearing a yellow star, whatever was written on it.

"In the end, Nerissa, what does your gesture achieve? Do you think for a moment that if you had indeed been a Jew you would have been treated with the same courtesy and compassion? Do you believe that if it had been Hakim – Hakim whose identity papers identify him as Hakim Benussan – that the same gallantry and bonhomie would have been extended to him?"

"I am sorry Vahan, you are surely right. I will stop wearing the star but I must tell you, my darling, that I feel better for having made some sort of statement, however futile it might have been."

Vahan remained silent. Was survival all that mattered? Simply looking at what was happening around him and making sympathetic comments when he got home to his family was, perhaps, not enough. Or was it? He was in turmoil.

Chapter 24

Petain and Mussolini

It took some time for Vahan to get his permit to leave Paris in order to go to live in Marseille – experiencing far more trouble with the Vichy authorities than with the Germans. However, eventually, the family did leave to go to Marseille, arriving at the Gare St. Charles only a few weeks before the allied landings in North Africa. That allied invasion resulted in the occupation by the Germans of most of the original Unoccupied Zone, whilst the Italians occupied the rest moving almost up to the line of the Rhone, though not including Marseille itself. The Asadourian family agent in Marseille, Raymond, was himself a Jew. He, however, came from an old family which had been French for generations. He had found them a light and airy flat in a rather shabby old building overlooking the Vieux Port itself. The arrival in the town of German soldiers some time after Vahan arrived, made little difference. As always it was the Vichy militia and the Vichy police that impinged on the population, not the enemy occupiers.

Vahan had seen very clearly during the thirties that there was an enormous difference between Nazi Germany and Fascist Italy when it came to their policy towards the Jews. Furthermore,

within a year of the original Armistice, it had also
became clear to him, as it did to many others,
that there was a similar difference between Vichy France and Fascist Italy. The arrests and the
deportation of the 14,000 Jews in Paris – French
citizens as well as foreign refugees – had shocked
him to the core and he had come to feel that the
only safe area for Hakim was in the Italian occupation zone. In his mind, right from the start of
his arrival in Marseille, he wanted to move on to
Nice, now well within the Italian zone.

On the issue of anti-semitism, Mussolini had a
far better record than the old and seemingly benevolent French Marshal Petain. Petain may have
had a patrician distaste for Laval and his out-and-
out policy of collaboration with the Germans, but
he never once lifted a finger, which he could easily have done, against the anti-semitic laws passed
by his governments under other prime ministers,
as well as Laval. Not a single one of those laws,
from the Statut des Juifs onwards, had been demanded by the Germans.

Laval has always had a bad press and perhaps
rightly so. Despite his many protestations that
he had no idea what the Germans were doing in
their deportations of the Jews, it seems impossible to accept that after seeing how old men and
children were included in the deportations, he
could still believe that it was similar to the STO
– the Service de Travail Obligatoire – which was
sending Frenchmen to work in the factories of the
Third Reich. However, Laval was at least consist-

ent. From the moment he came to prominence in the 1920's and long before Hitler came to power, he was a believer in establishing good relations with Germany. He always wanted France to align itself with Germany rather than with Great Britain. His defence is encapsulated in his statement issued from his prison cell in 1945 before he was executed, which ended –

"Regimes follow one another, and revolutions and changes of fortune take place – but geography remains unchanged. We will be neighbours of Germany, whatever happens, for ever."

Petain might have looked good with his white patrician moustache, whilst Laval looked like a crook – but Petain's defeatist corruption was in the end far more sinister with graver consequences.

On the other hand, in contrast to the indifferent Petain, Mussolini had said publicly, a propos the mounting Nazi hysteria – "National pride has no need for the delirium of race." Indeed at no time, until his fall from power in 1943, did Mussolini ever indulge in any of the vicious anti-semitism so prevalent elsewhere in Europe.

Everyone was accordingly well aware that the Italian military commanders in their occupied zone were not in sympathy with German anti-semitism. They openly thwarted Vichy laws in their own zone in the south of France. Their peers in the areas they administered in the Balkans were equally unsympathetic to the Ustasha – the Croat fascists – and were able to save many

Jews who would otherwise have met the fate of deportation. Unlike Vichy France, Italy was determined to be protective of all its citizens, Jew as well as non-Jew, in areas administered by them.

Mussolini paid only lip-service to German demands for legal action against the Jews of Italy; demands which the Germans never needed to make to Petain, as the Vichy government was in any case, on its own initiative, passing all the necessary laws and enforcing them. Despite the bland assurances given by Mussolini to his allies, he turned a blind eye to the manner in which his officials were thwarting the will of the Germans on this issue. Mussolini's regime – at least before he fell – did its best to try and sabotage the Final Solution in Croatia, Greece and Tunisia. The Italians also provided a safe haven for Jews in their zone of Vichy France.

During 1943 Vichy stepped up its persecution and the French police made mass arrests in the old unoccupied zone. These were French arrests made by French police under French Vichy statutes – no German soldiers were involved. But in their zone Italian troops were on several occasions ordered to block railroad tracks to prevent the passage of trainloads of deportees. In Nice itself the Italian Consul-General informed the local French prefect that he was not to enforce the Vichy anti-semitic laws in his zone. He also made it clear that there was to be no stamping of the word 'Jew' on identity cards. The Italian military commander of the Nice area told the local police chief there that any French policeman detaining a Jew illegally would himself be arrested.

All this so incensed the Germans that Ribbentrop went to Rome specifically to remonstrate with Mussolini. He denied that Italy was doing anything to annul or delay the anti-Jewish round-ups – although he knew perfectly well that that was untrue. Ostentatiously in front of Ribbentrop he appointed an Inspector to check on Racial Policy in the Italian zone. The man appointed did not even bother to leave Rome and Mussolini said not a word. Vichy meanwhile continued in all the zones to arrest and deport French Jews as well as foreign refugees.

Vahan and his family had arrived in Marseille in October 1942 and several weeks later the Germans marched into the zone following the allied invasion of North Africa. The French fleet was scuttled in Toulon to prevent it falling into the hands of the Germans. This was perhaps the only promise that Admiral Darlan and the Vichy leaders ever kept. In January 1943, before Vahan had even managed to arrange for a school for Hakim, a large organised round-up of Jews was arranged to 'cleanse' Marseille of 'undesirable elements'. It was decided that the rather seedy streets and old crumbling buildings surrounding the sides of the Vieux Port should be dynamited.

Vahan was forewarned about the coming operation and he had already moved out of the flat to live for a short time with his friend and agent Raymond, though he too was vulnerable despite coming from an old French-born family. Directed almost entirely by Vichy officials, over 10,000 French police, some in uniform and some in plainclothes, gathered for the occasion from all over France and took part in the round-ups. Forty thousand people had their identities checked, and in the end almost 2,000 Jews, including whole families with their children, were deported.

If smiling at a young German soldier who offered up his seat in the metro to a young lady was the most moderate end of the 'collaboration' graph, Marseille in January 1943 was at the extreme opposite end. The old twisting streets and shabby but evocative buildings to each side of the Vieux Port were ruthlessly dynamited after the round-up. The arrest of French Jews in Marseille at last and for the first time in the whole Vichy story, aroused a muted and pathetically weak reaction from the Catholic hierarchy. A Cardinal wrote to the Chief Rabbi in Paris stating that surely it must have all been a matter of confusion. But only a few days later, French police arrested and arranged for the deportation of 48 Jewish children hidden in orphanages in Paris.

The decision that Vahan was to take much later was heavily influenced by the discussions he had with Raymond the night before he, Nerissa and Hakim left for Nice. It started, as so often, with Nerissa raising an issue which in her mind was a purely intellectual exercise, but which to her inevitable distress became heavily emotional to everyone else in the room.

"My dear Raymond, your family has been French for generations – pre-revolutionary I believe you said – where then exactly does your Jewishness reside.?"

"I'm not sure that the question has any validity – but nevertheless it is a problem in a way," said Vahan, joining in. "It can't reside in the religion surely. I've never ever seen you go to the Synagogue."

"No, you are quite right. I have no belief whatsoever in all that intolerant monotheistic fantasy, except perhaps as a historical record. So what is it? It is certainly something which I have never questioned in myself. It is – to put it simplistically – a part of my identity, a part of what makes me – me. I was born a Jew and I know that my parents had themselves been born Jewish – but of course French as well. Surely there is no need to quantify it in some way. It's all part of me."

"Nevertheless, Raymond, what does it mean now."

Ah, well, here is the paradox. Before the war and when I was first contacted by your father Vahan, I lived my life, as did my family, in almost completely disregard of the Jewish part of my identity. It meant nothing to me except as an old historical accident. But oddly enough the persecution by Vichy has slowly but surely brought out that part of my identity more and more."

"Yes, I can understand that. Something similar happened with us earlier in the century. Armenians who had been good Ottoman citizens, prepared to be loyal to the empire that ruled over so many different races, became, as it were, more Armenian and more nationalist the more they were persecuted."

"Well it all came to a head for me in June of last year. The Americans were still neutral. Travel to the USA was still possible on neutral ships. Your father – Garabed – wrote to me and urged me to take my family to America, or at least to send my two children. He offered to give such assistance as he could. I spent hours of agonised debate, but in the end decided against it. I wrote back to your father saying that I would remain, whatever happens, a Frenchman till I died. That was easy. But if the French state legally rejects me and my family – do I have the right to make that same decision for my children. Oh Vahan I was wrong – I was wrong – I should have sent my kids away."

The conversation went on all night, but the issue was left unresolved. Vahan and his family left the next morning. Travelling by train they arrived in Nice, where the Italians were still in charge. Vahan took a small flat in the old town and at last got Hakim into the local state lycee. The boy had not been to school since they had left Paris four months previously. Hakim was now over twelve. He looked nothing like the fair-haired Nerissa or Vahan's solid figure. He was dark and had oriental features. This was a matter which would have had no significance at all in almost any other circumstances – but which in the extraordinary circumstances of occupied Vichy France turned out to be fatal.

It was Xmas Day almost a year later that Vahan heard that Raymond, his wife and two children had been arrested and been deported to a French internment camp, and from there in the New Year to Auschwitz. They were never heard of again.

Chapter 25

The Partisans

Conrad remained in Rome throughout the nine months of the German occupation. Protected by Giancarlo's PCI toughs, he witnessed the horrors and the brutalities visited on the unfortunate Roman citizens during those extraordinary months. He continued to wander round the city, no longer in uniform but with his arm still in a sling and with bandages and an eye-patch over his left eye. As the Allied armies approached, worries about the incomparable heritage of the art and architecture of the Eternal City surfaced. Various attempts by the Vatican to put pressure on the two opposing military commanders, finally resulted in a patched up agreement to give Rome the status of an 'open city'. On the allied side the one or two inaccurate bombing raids they had made on the railway junctions and workshops had caused such an outcry that any military benefit was clearly not going to be worth the political fall-out in any case. On the German side, accepting the concept of the open city meant that the important railroad connections to the troops fighting south of the city would remain intact, free of any attempt to dislocate them by bombing or direct attacks by sabotage.

A part of Conrad's duties during this period

was to monitor how far this agreement was being kept by the Germans. He dutifully reported any infringements, not that there were in fact many. Not much notice was taken by the Allied command in any case, but what was undoubtedly more useful was the regular information gathered by all Conrad's contacts about the movements through the city of German troops – infringements or not.

During this period, between the Italian surrender and the final arrival of the Allied forces in June 1944, the famous early Christian catacombs housed a large number of fugitive Jews. The Jewish population of Rome had not been persecuted whilst Mussolini was still in power. He had nodded in supine assent to Hitler and German demands where the Jews were concerned – but had never taken any serious steps. So, while Vichy was passing all sorts of anti-semitic laws and enforcing them, nothing like that was happening in Italy. A forced registration of Jews similar to that in Vichy France had indeed been reluctantly promulgated, but neither Mussolini nor most Italian civil officials made any real attempt to enforce it. Most Italian Jews came up with altered papers and even forged birth certificates, if they bothered to register at all. Above all and in stark contrast to Vichy France, the Jews found that they had the covert sympathy of most people around them. Denunciations, tale-telling or virulent anti-semitism was rare.

But once Mussolini fell, and the Wehrmacht

flooded into the city, things changed overnight. Fortunately, the failure, deliberate or not, to register the Jews, meant that the Gestapo and the other occupation authorities did not know who were Jews or where they lived. Nevertheless, on one well-documented occasion, an attempt was made for a round-up of Rome's Jews. Not a single Italian policeman was involved or collaborated with the attempt. Shouts and screams from the first apartments raided alerted anyone living nearby. All the Jews living within earshot clambered down the fire escapes or across the roofs to seek refuge. Those not nearby were warned by neighbours as to what was happening and also sought refuge where they could. Rome was willing to hide most of them.

The Germans never had any idea how to placate or live with a state or a people whom they had defeated and, accordingly, considered inferior. They had ruined their chances in Soviet Russia by spurning Ukrainian separatists, who had initially looked on the arrival of the German army as liberators. They acted in the same way towards Russian peasants who also had no reason to feel any loyalty towards Stalin's regime. They ended up uniting all the varied peoples of the Soviet Union in deep hatred of them and their regime. They acted equally ham-fistedly in Italy. Even though they were supposed to be allied to the Fascist government set up in the north, they treated all Italians, of whatever political persuasion, with a cold contempt. The result, once again, was a slowly simmering hatred that built up against them and their fascist lackeys. This manifested itself in the rise of the Partisan movement which harried the Germans and disrupted their war machine.

Meanwhile Mussolini was trying to run a Fascist Republic in the north. His black-shirted militia was bitterly anti-partisan. The Partisans on their part turned their attention more and more against the fascists. The result was an extraordinary Civil War which raged between Italians, whilst all around them a conventional war was going on between complete foreigners over control of their soil. The Partisans themselves were not a homogeneous whole. There were groups linked to the Royal government in the south; groups with purely local connections and opposed both to the communists and the royalists; one or two groups who even set up and declared independent Republics; groups connected to the communist PCI.

Nicolai and his friend Count Pietro talked and analysed the situation for hours over bottles of their ever-decreasing wine cellars. They were unable to arrive at a clear decision on their own positions until one day, walking past the main station in Florence, they witnessed a shocking example of what the country had come to.

A long train that was carrying Italian regular soldiers being held as prisoners of war was standing in the station. It was guarded by a detachment of Fascist black-shirts on the platform and two German-manned machine-gun posts on the top of the carriages. The Italian soldiers, most of them uncomprehending young conscripts press-ganged into the Royal army, were calling out for water. A party of women pushed into the open station – the building itself was in ruins from previous bombing – bringing pitchers of water and even some scarce bread.

As Nicolai and Pietro watched, both the Fascist blackshirts and the German guards shouted at the women to get back. The women came doggedly on and were already handing up the water jugs to the outstretched hands from within the train when the machine guns on the roof opened fire, followed by massed rifle shots from the militia on the platform. With screams of terror the women fled, but more than thirty lay wounded or dead on the platform. The young men who had been shooting stared, equally stunned and uncomprehending at what they had just done, and made no move to help those women feebly crawling about, bleeding from gunshot wounds. There and then, as they finally ran forward to help together with other civilians standing nearby, Nicolai and Pietro decided to join the Partisans. Within a few days they had settled their affairs, left home and begun to live rough with the Partisans.

For the next year Sima dealt as well as she could with the estate business, travelling to the Veneto when necessary. But for most of the time she continued to live in Florence with her mother-in-law, neither of them of course having any idea where Nicolai might be. Nicolai and Pietro kept together and moved from one group to another, but in the end were working with a group that recognised the authority of the Committee of National Liberation set up in Rome those many months before.

Chapter 26

Hakim

In September 1943 after Mussolini had fallen from power, and following the botched surrender of the Badoglio government, the Germans marched into that part of Vichy France previously occupied by the Italians. This now coincided with the worst excesses of the Vichy regime. The obnoxious and fanatically anti-semitic Darnand took over control of the notorious Vichy Milice. Jew-hunting became an obsession and went on unabated right up to the very day of the liberation of Paris.. The final deportation convoy – the 67th – left the French internment camp of Drancy in July taking 51 Jews to Buchenwald. It left only a few days before the Germans fled from Paris. Altogether about 67,000 Jews were deported from Drancy alone, and, of those, over 11,000 were children. Not one of the children survived.

In Nice, during those months between the departure of the Italians right up to the liberation of Paris and the allied landings near Toulon in the summer of 1944, the Milice roamed the streets in their sinister black Citroens. Sitting in their sleek long cars they would watch balefully as the citizenry passed by on the pavements. Quite randomly and without any warning they would suddenly open the doors jump out and pounce on some individual – boy – youth – old man –

and drive them to their headquarters. There they would be interrogated and their papers checked. If Jewish identity could be established, he would be arrested. It was then completely arbitrary and a matter of luck as to what would happen next. If it was a boy, he might get away with a beating, but, more often than not, it would be deportation to Drancy. No German would be involved either in the initial arrest or, until later, in the eventual deportation.

Hakim of course was included in the papers of Vahan and Nerissa showing them to be Turkish citizens. But as the days passed both Vahan and Nerissa became more and more nervous for his safety. It soon became common knowledge that the Vichy Milice were now taking men suspected of being Jewish to their headquarters and making them strip to see if they were circumcised. Hakim, of course, was.

Vichy, and all its officials, were deeply guilty of a major moral lapse, far worse than anything of which the Catholics and the Right had accused the old Third Republic; but the ordinary citizen now witnessing the sight of screaming children clinging on to their parents as they were led away, instinctively recognised the evil of what was happening – an evil which the Catholic hierarchy almost entirely failed to see.

It was an irony that left entirely to his own still unformed instincts, Hakim, whose mother-tongue was Turkish and who spoke both Armenian and Turkish well, would probably have chosen – if such a choice had been open to him – to have been an Armenian like his adopted parents. But at the same time Hakim had not forgotten his regular attendances at the local Synagogue with his father Joshua all those years ago. How could he forget the pride and pleasure of walking hand in hand holding his father's hand and being warmly welcomed by other men with their boys in that weekly ritual. Once he had come of age, Hakim had been made by Vahan to attend the Synagogue and receive instruction in Judaism. But at the age of 12 what was important to him, as to any average boy of that age, was his parent's love – not theology or race. Though he knew well that his parents loved him, he could never shake that sneaking devastating feeling that perhaps they would have loved him even more if he had been born Armenian.

Hakim had lost both his parents when he was four years old. Oddly he had no clear memory of his mother Rachel. From about the age of two onwards, as an active toddler, his memories of her were inevitably bound up with the Asadourian apartment and the cheerful and cosy kitchen where he would play on the floor around her feet. Nerissa was nearly always present, and would occasionally play with him when Rachel was particularly busy. In this way his memory of 'mother' as a concept was always muddled between the two women. His memory of his father was sharper even though he had seen him far less and only at the weekends. Above all he never confused Vahan and Joshua.

For Hakim it was never just the classic problem of the adopted child. Vahan and Nerissa were both excellent parents in that respect and Hakim knew with a complete inner certainty that he was loved by them equally, as if they had been his biological parents. But every child, can never have enough reinforcement of parental love, even where they have it to the full. The problem in his case was not parental love, it was the requirement by society – his peer group – his teachers – his friends – that he should declare his identity. Society could not, and still does not, accept the unique nature of every person's identity. Everyone has to be categorised into some group or another for the average person to feel comfortable.

So, what was Hakim's identity? It is almost always a meaningless question when one is asked 'what do you really feel to be your identity deep down.' Like everyone else in the world Hakim had only one unique identity, made up of a myriad of experiences and factors that had shaped him from the moment he was born. Unfortunately it was not only the Nazis or the Vichy Milice who believed that 'deep down inside' everyone there is just one identity trait that really matters. For the nation-state enthusiast it is your sense of nation. For the religious enthusiast it is your religious beliefs. For those who believe in significant racial differences it is your race. They all want to reduce identity in its fascinating varied forms to one single most significant affiliation.

Most people would understand without any difficulty that Hakim could have many different 'allegiances' – all of varied strengths and all changeable – as the circumstances of his life changed. For the Vichy Milice however – indeed behind the whole ethos of the Vichy government – lay the clear and inescapable belief that Hakim had one overriding identity – that of being a Jew.

Hakim himself, prior to his experiences in Vichy France, used to refer to himself as having a Jewish background. Paradoxically, the more dangerous it became to be a Jew, the more he accepted that part of his identity. The headmaster of the school which Hakim attended in Nice, and indeed most of his classmates, were aware, without being certain, that Hakim was Jewish. On this occasion that knowledge was used positively.

The Vichy Milice in Nice poked their noses in everywhere and one Monday, early in the morning, they decided to mount a raid on the school at which Hakim was a pupil. They knew that schools, convents, charitable houses and institutions of all kinds were now sheltering Jewish children, as ordinary French people became more aware of what was happening. Darnand decided early in 1944 that the authorities must try to weed the hidden children out, starting with the schools. State schools were easier to enter and bully. That morning the Milice arrived at the school and informed the headmaster that at the morning assembly they would be demanding to see the papers of all the boys, and that they would be taking away anyone who did not have satisfactory papers or who appeared to be an 'undesirable element' – this was the current euphemism for being Jewish.

The boys had already begun filtering in. The headmaster flashed through his mind all the boys he could think of who might be in danger; he thought of several including Hakim. Excusing himself from the police, who were assisting the Milice in case formal arrests were necessary, he hurried to Hakim's classroom. Some of the boys had already arrived and were discussing excitedly the presence of the police and the Milice in the grounds and at the front gate. Speaking quickly, and anxious to get on to the other classrooms on the same errand, he spoke to the four boys already there –

"Boys – do you know Hakim Asadourian?"

"Yes sir, certainly sir, he is in our class."

"Do you know from which direction he comes in the mornings on his way to school"

"Er...I do sir. He comes down the road from the old market and across the Square."

"Good! Now look, can you all go out by the back door and try to find Hakim before he arrives. Go round to the front entrance and fan out from there. Tell him that he is not to come to school today and that he should go straight back home and stay there. He should tell his father what has happened here and what I have said. But listen carefully, it is very important that all four of you are back here for roll-call even if you can't find him."

The four boys crept out by the back door to the kitchens, ran round to the front and sauntering past the men at the front gate, went off in search of Hakim. One of the boys very soon saw Hakim passing by the old market, swinging his satchel and walking with a friend whom he had met on his way to school and chatting away at the top of his voice in his rather accented French. Although only twelve, he was aware of the danger that stalked the streets, but then, he was only twelve, and swinging his satchel and talking with animation seemed so natural. The boy who first saw him was also a friend. He told Hakim all that the headmaster had said, and he warned him of what was happening at the school. Hakim hovered a little uncertain of what to do. But then a second boy came up who was not a particular friend and said -

"Hey Jewboy, you'd better run off home to Mummy or you might get your little prick inspected and cut off.".

Hakim blushed red and was about to shout an insult back. However, by then his two friends were already threatening to pick a fight there and then in the street and were loudly remonstrating with the other lad, who had the grace to mutter '"I'm sorry, I'm sorry, but see here, there is danger at school you really must go home." Hakim looked down then shook hands all round and turned to return home.

This incident was probably the last straw which

pushed Vahan over the edge into a decision affecting himself that he had been contemplating for some time since arriving in Nice. Already angry at being forced out of Paris to Marseille and then from there to Nice, he felt that he could no longer remain uninvolved in all that was happening around him. First he decided that Hakim was not to go back to school, but was to stay at home and be taught by Nerissa as best she could. Furthermore he also insisted that there were to be no excursions into the streets – none at all. Hakim's exercise was to be limited to running about in the little garden at the back of the building. If there was any vital necessity for an appearance on the streets Hakim was to wear short trousers with long socks like the younger schoolboys. Finally Nerissa was to cut his lovely long curly black hair – it was all to come off except for just a thin covering so that he didn't look as if he had some disease.

Nerissa exploded, backed up by Hakim who was close to tears as Vahan uncharacteristically drove on, laying down rules without giving anyone any time to object. The little family then argued all the rest of that same day that Hakim had returned from going to school. In the night, after Hakim had gone to bed, sitting together in their bedroom, Nerissa finally calmed down.

"Very well Vahan, I don't agree, I think you have gone over the top, but as you are so convinced I will go along with your wishes. I'll cut Hakim's hair tomorrow and see if I can widen his old school shorts so that he can wear them. But look why all these rules now? Why this careful parade of do's and don'ts at this particular moment?"

"My dear nothing is decided for sure as yet, but, coupled with this close escape, I have made a decision that…"

"What do you mean close escape? The headmaster was overreacting. Hakim's papers are clear – he is a citizen of the Turkish Republic and is here in France as the son of an undisputedly Christian couple, Marseille is full of Armenians and the Germans haven't touched one – why should they."

"Oh Nerissa, Nerissa – you assume that everything will always go forward logically, naturally and lawfully. That headmaster was right. Most of the boys in the school, and certainly those in his class, know that Hakim is a Jew. The only papers that he has for himself is his Turkish nufus which clearly includes the word 'Jew'. His name on our own passport is different to ours. Do you think for a moment that the Milice would not learn the truth? Do you think that they would take any notice of legal papers once they had seen that he was circumcised?"

"Very well, very well, don't go on about it. But why all the laying down of rules now, when you are always around anyway? You're up to something. You're cooking up some idea, I can tell."

"Nerissa, my soul, I have been thinking about something for some time. But it wasn't until today when my son was forced to sneak back home frightened and humiliated that I have made up my mind. For nearly four years I have slunk about on the fringes of French society doing nothing – nothing at all – about the situation in which we all find ourselves. Great events are happening all about us and…"

"Oh my God, Vahan my soul, what are you getting at. This is not your quarrel, we just have to sit it out. Isn't it enough that you survived the horrors of the Great War and the massacres in which your own people were directly involved. Why are you now …"

"My love, my love, it is partly that which is driving me on. I did so little during the events of `1915' when so many of us were so passive in the face of evil. I can no longer sit about and let things like what happened today to my son pass by without taking some sort of action. I am going to see if I can be of any use to the Resistance."

"Male pride and arrogance! You're not French and you're almost fifty and already well past military age. Your family is not really being threatened and we need you, we need you to be with us."

"I know, I know. Look, it's unlikely that anyone is going to ask me to do anything dangerous or requiring physical strength. I just intend making it known that I am available if they need anything. I have a friend who I am sure has some sort of part-time connection with some elements of the local Resistance movement."

"But…"

"My mind is made up. I promise you, my love, that I will not volunteer for anything like sabotage or involving murder. I just have to do something, even if it's only largely symbolic. I did nothing against evil in 1915 – I am not going to sit back and keep a low profile again when the same thing is happening 25 years later"

"But Vahan, Vahan, my soul, there was nothing you could have done in 1915 and there is nothing you could or should do now either. Things happen. All we can do is the best of what we are capable".

Nerissa, beginning to get into a panic as she looked into Vahan's clear brown eyes went on, beginning to get a little hysterical.

"It's male pride – oh my God Vahan it's male arrogance that is forcing you to take some sort of public stance. Honour…It's all nonsense! Rubbish! The only thing that is important in life is love – you don't have to stand up for some concept of morality to show that. Vahan…"

"So, my beloved what was it that made you wear the yellow star all those months ago in Paris. Was female pride somehow more acceptable?"

At this, Nerissa finally hung her head. There was a stillness as silent tears fell down her cheeks. But as she looked up at her beloved husband, to her surprise, she saw tears in his eyes as well.

"I'm sorry, my love, I have to act. It's the hunting party – my God yes – Some time or another I have to stand up against the hunting party…"

"What the devil; are you talking about Vahan?"

"Never mind my love – it's not important – all you need to know is that I love you. I have always loved you. Come Nerissa … come to me …

And so it was, that within a few months of each other, Vahan joined the French resistance, just as his brother-in-law, Count Nicolai Androv, joined the Italian Partisans.

Chapter 27

Florence

On the 5th June 1944 American troops at last entered Rome without any further fighting. The Germans retreated across the Tiber bridges all of which remained intact. Marshall Kesselring had struck an informal bargain with the Allies. The whole city including the bridges would be left inviolate as long as there were no air strikes or direct action against the Germans as they abandoned the area.

The Allies had agreed and then given instructions to all their agents in the city to put pressure on those Partisan groups to which they were attached to comply with the arrangements and to refrain from attacking the retreating Germans. Conrad had the hardest task of all those agents. His PCI group was the toughest of the various Communist groups operating in the city, and it took a lot of ardent persuasion to prevent them going out with a view to disrupting the German retreat.

With the appearance of the Americans, Conrad's operation was over, and shortly after their arrival he rejoined his original unit. His temporary rank as acting Captain was confirmed and he went forward with the advancing Allied forces as they slowly moved north towards the next German defensive position – the Gothic Line. By now the invasion of Normandy had taken place and all the Western Allied effort was concentrated on the Battle for France. The Italian campaign became a side issue.

The focus of this side-show now became the city of Florence. The last possible defensive position before the Gothic Line was the River Arno which flowed through Florence and out to the sea beyond Pisa. There seemed to be no way that Florence, right in between the two competing armies, could be saved from devastating destruction. There was clearly yet again a problem. In the month of May, there was a bombing raid intended to hit the major railroad hub that ran through the city. It so happened that this raid scored a direct hit on a Teatro where a rehearsal of Mozart's Cosi Fan Tutti was taking place. This highlighted an important fact about Florence. It was undoubtedly one of the greatest centres of European art – medieval and renaissance – containing buildings, bridges and artefacts of priceless beauty.

There was no Pope or Catholic public opinion to put pressure for any accommodation. But in this case the two enemy sides took a direct initiative themselves. Kesselring declared Florence to be an 'open city' on the 23rd June. This time it was some Italian Partisans who denounced the declaration. In their underground newssheets they urged Partisan groups in the city not to stop their activities against German interests. Bombs were set off at the railroad station on two occasions as well as the Excelsior Hotel, used largely by German officers, which was also attacked. Once again Conrad, together with a colleague who had been with him in Rome, was asked to infiltrate into the city to contact the specific Resistance group which had been causing all the trouble. This time it was the Autonomi – a monarchist group on the Right. They agreed to welcome the Allied agents and to facilitate their entry into the city. Conrad was instructed to remain with this group in an effort to persuade them to cease taking reprisals against the Germans, who were clearly making plans to abandon the city.

Getting into Florence was a good deal more difficult than getting into Rome had been the year before. But this particular Partisan group were efficient and just as ruthless and thuggish as the Communists in Rome. Creeping along water-courses, through abandoned suburbs and moving from woods to gardens, Conrad finally arrived with his guards behind the German lines south of the city. He was exhausted. The short-wave radio he was carrying was not light and it had had to be carefully manhandled as they passed through and along streams and sewers. Whether the Monarchists were more amenable than the Communists, or Conrad's powers of persuasion had developed, the fact was that after his arrival no further Autonomi attacks were launched. It looked as if Florence was going to escape any major destruction.

By the 4th August the Allied armies had

reached the southern side of the city, on the south side of the River Arno, which was now the only major obstacle between the two armies. Then on the 11th August, the German commander at last ordered an evacuation. That morning, as the German units began to move out, the great bell of the Palazzo Vecchio began to toll. This had always been the traditional signal in the city for an insurrection. Whether there was any real danger or not from the citizenry, the German units still on the south side of the River began to panic. The knowledge that they were the only units left on the wrong side of the river, coupled with the mournful and dramatic sound of the tolling bell, caused the unfortunate outrage that then took place despite everyone's efforts so far. They poured back across the bridges and then blew them all up, except for the Ponte Vecchio, which, as it had shops on both sides from end to end, could not be used for any large vehicles. The Ponte alle Grazie had been built in 1237. The Ponte Garraia with its beautiful camel-hump shape dated from 1330.

Finally after retiring from south of the river, the Germans gradually moved on north and out of the main city. The Allied soldiers did not move in for some days and during that period there was a power vacuum in the city filled for a time by the Partisans. On the third day, as small Allied units filtered into the city Conrad took the plunge and at last decided to make a visit to the Palazzo Maggi.

The Countess Natalya Androvna, Nicolai's mother, had had two sisters and two brothers. She was the eldest child in the Naritsyn family. During the warm summer months of those seemingly relaxed years at the end of the nineteenth century, Count Naritsyn, his wife and all his children, would move from one fashionable European spa to another before returning to St. Petersburg for the Autumn season. Natalya's two sisters were born within the following two years. There was then a long gap until the birth of her two brothers.

Both of her sisters married before her – both picking up the most eligible of husbands. The elder – Varvara – found her man during a month spent in the spa at Marienbad, becoming the Countess Berchtold. Her husband, quite a bit older than her, was a Viennese aristocrat with political ambitions who moved in fairly high circles in the Hapsburg court. In due course, he became the foreign minister of the Austro-Hungarian Empire and was in that vitally important position at the time of the assassination of Franz Ferdinand - the heir to the throne - in Sarajevo in 1914. For most people, their mistakes or misjudgements could often give rise to serious consequences for themselves or even for others. But in the case of this admirably polite and courteous gentleman, who had ambled along with the rest of the aristocracy of Old Europe from one fashionable watering-hole to another, his mistakes and errors of judgement had given rise to one of the most catastrophic of consequences affecting the whole world.

Of course no one statesman, no one monarch or country, could be held responsible alone for the seismic catastrophe that was the Great War. But in the balance, and with innumerable 'ifs' and 'buts', the one power that consistently sought war from the start, albeit wanting only a local one, was Austria-Hungary, and this mild gentleman was that power's foreign policy controller at the time.

The younger of the three Naritsyn sisters – Sofia – first met her man – the Conte Maggi – during a house party held for the purpose of hunting some bird or another at the Scottish home of a milord. This encounter had been followed two weeks later by a further meeting with the same ardent Italian Count in Baden-Baden.

Sofia had also married well – that is from the point of view of a somewhat impoverished Russian aristocratic family. The Conte Maggi was not a young man at the time of their first meeting on the game moors of Scotland. Still, he had fallen deeply in love with Sofia and had arranged to follow her that same summer when he found out that the family were moving on to Baden-Baden. Whereas Varvara had been wooed in French and German, Sofia was wooed in French and English. Maggi, unlike Berchtold had no political ambitions. He held considerable land holdings throughout the Veneto and dotted about the North Italian plain east of Verona. He loved the countryside and, though not farming himself, took a direct personal interest in his estates and the farms and villages of his tenants. He often lived on his estate, even though he had palazzi, one in Venice and one in Florence.

Natalya was still unmarried, at the very ripe age of 24, when she first met her man – not in the high spots of aristocratic Europe but back in Russia, in Moscow, where she was staying for a few months with relatives. Her husband Count Androv, was a bit like his brother-in-law Maggi in being interested in his land. He lived permanently on his estate in the south near the river Don. He directly managed the land, exploiting the forests and developing some small local industries including a paper-mill. He had his son – Nicolai – educated at the local village school where he installed an excellent schoolteacher from Moscow and paid his wages. Of course Nicolai had home tutors as well and before attending school had had an English governess. Natalya had been wooed in French and Russian.

The three sisters were all now widows and were living together in one of the Conte Maggi's palazzi – the one he had modernised in Florence. Count Berchtold had died in Vienna in the late twenties after completing and publishing his memoirs, which reiterated at considerable length the simple statement that none of it had been his fault. The old Count Androv had died long before on the Eastern front during the Great War and Natalya's two younger brothers had also not survived their father by very long.

Neither of the two younger sisters – the Countesses Berchtold or Maggi – had had any children. Natalya had two boys. Her eldest son, Nicolai, now Count Androv, had married Karekin Avakian's eldest daughter Sima and had come to Italy to act as manager for Conte Maggi's estates. He had got on well with the Count and Nicolai's efficiency had allowed the old Count to indulge in his favourite pastime of hunting and riding round his estates chatting to all his tenants and generally being a benevolent landlord. He could, of course, afford to be, as all the hard and more unpopular decisions were now taken by Nicolai. The old Count had died after a bad fall from his horse, just before the outbreak of the Second World War.

On the death of Conte Maggi, the three sisters decided to move and live together in the renovated Palazzo Maggi in Florence. Varvara, the Countess Berchtold had been living on her own in Vienna, whilst Natalya had been living with Nicolai and Sima in their house on the Veneto estate. The Palazzo had been reorganised into three separate apartments, so they were able to have an apartment each.

Conrad had never actually met the Contessa Maggi or her sister the Countess Berchtold, but

Sima, the wife of Count Nicolai Androv, was his Aunt. Thus Natalya, the Countess Androvna, the third of the sisters, was his Aunt's mother-in-law. He had fond memories of meeting Sima and Nicolai fairly regularly at Milan station during their pre-war summer trips to Istanbul. They had always come with something for the boys, and he recalled the last occasion in the summer of 1939 when a whole box of peaches had been delivered.

The Palazzo Maggi was a modest three-storey building neither very old nor in a particularly fashionable part of the town. Conrad had been careful not to endanger anyone by going there when he first arrived. But even now the situation was still unstable. Whereas almost all the Germans had now departed, no major force of Allied troops had yet entered the town. Accordingly, Conrad returned to his favourite disguise with his arm in a sling and wearing an eye-patch, and, of course, still in civilian clothes. He rang the bell at the large and imposing front door. A voice eventually called out through a grill in a small window next to the door –

"Who is it?"

"My name is Conrad Bridgeman, Signora. I am English. Can you please tell the Countess Androvna that I would like to visit her."

"What do you want?"

"I am a relative. Please just tell her that I am here and that I am Madame Sima's nephew."

There was a long silence as the concierge, or whoever had answered, went off to seek some instructions. This was no surprise to Conrad who thought they might not open to him at all. These were dangerous times and most civilians remained strictly indoors and kept a low profile. Nicolai's mother had never met him, and it was perfectly reasonable that they would be suspicious of this rough-looking character with an eye-patch and his arm in a sling.

However, eventually the door opened. A middle-aged woman dressed completely in black looked sternly out at Conrad, and then motioned him in without a word. Carefully locking the door behind her, she proceeded up the marble stairs. These began at the end of a short, dark stone-paved hallway with a door to one side. This was ajar and led into a room or rooms from which the woman had obviously emerged. Conrad who had a quick eye for details noted the corridor alongside the stairs, that went on to a door at the far end that clearly must lead out into a garden or a patio. The stairs led up to a first floor with one door leading into an apartment. They went further up the stairs leading on to a second and third floor, where they finally stopped.

Standing at the top of the stairs waiting for them was the eldest of the three sisters – Natalya, the Countess Androvna. Conrad tried a shy smile and extended his hand to the Countess.

"And how are your dear mother and father?"

"My mother Olga and my father Harry are both well, but being with the British army, I have not seen them for two years," Conrad replied and tried another smile.

At this Natalya herself beamed and stepped forward taking hold of Conrad's hand and giving him a kiss on both cheeks. The stern black-clad woman who had brought him up the stairs now also grinned, nodding her head up and down vigorously in delight. Conrad was led into the sunny top floor apartment, while the concierge, or maid, introduced to him as Giuseppina, was sent down to fetch the two other sisters – the Contessa Berchtold and the Contessa Maggi.

After two years of war, Conrad had a particularly wonderful four hours in the company of these three grand old ladies from a previous age. All three were already in their seventies, but all three were well-preserved, though, due to all the current shortages, looking rather frail. They adored having a handsome young man, not more than 21, as company and, despite his shabby clothes, Conrad made a great impression. They offered him refreshments rather diffidently. Conrad, however, aware of the terrible shortages of food and the dire straits into which Italian civilians were being forced, declined politely. Eventually he took a glass of liquor as they were obviously so anxious that he should take something. He explained what he was doing and why he was there; he explained about the arm in a sling and the eye-patch; he talked nostalgically about the family; he talked and talked and they listened with obvious great pleasure, and asked him no awkward questions. After two years of living in rough, purely male conditions, Conrad loved the whole atmosphere of the Palazzo – a love which never left him.

Once the city was fully occupied by the Allies, Conrad reported to his unit when it, too, arrived in the city. Once again, he was back in uniform. His clothes and personal effects had been brought along. His Intelligence unit remained in Florence for two weeks and, on most days when he was free, Conrad tried to visit the three sisters. He never went there without taking something from the rations which he had scrounged. On one memorable occasion, he managed to get a whole bag of rice which he handed to Giuseppina, who did all the cooking for the three Contesse who always took their main meal together, usually in the first floor apartment belonging to Sofia, the Countess Maggi. On two occasions he even went out, walking slowly with the Countess Natalya clinging onto his arm. Conrad fell in love – with the three widowed old ladies – with all the beauty and the art around him – and with the city.

Two days before his unit was due to move out, the three Countesses absolutely insisted on his coming to a dinner at the Palazzo. Conrad arrived in full dress uniform. Dinner was very frugal – a pastino in brodo, a very thin brodo indeed – followed by a risotto – but what was in it other than the rice was difficult to work out. However, the whole meal, served by a now attentive and cheerful Giuseppina, was presented with real panache and elegance. The table was laid with lovely glasses, there was a good red wine, which each of the ladies took a small and delicate sip from the bottom of their cut glasses and, glowing in the darkened room, were candles in silver holders.

When he left that night, Conrad did something he had never done before – he took the hand of each of the ladies, bowed over it and kissed it without any self-consciousness. They adored it, and all insisted that once the war was over he should return and visit them again.

Chapter 28

Dr. Grimaud

It was easy enough for Vahan simply to stand up in his sitting room and state firmly to his wife and son that he had had enough of being pushed from pillar to post and that he was going to join the Resistance – the Maquis – as it was now called. It was a good deal more difficult to put this into effect. Vahan knew few people in Nice whom he could approach. There was a small Armenian community centred around a church in the old quarter of the city. But the Armenians, refugees from the massacres of 1915, kept a low profile. Almost all of them were now full French citizens. However, as a community, they steered a middle course through the dilemma facing everybody. There were no Armenian collaborators or denouncers, and generally they did not support Vichy, but equally there were no Armenian Résistants either.

All Vahan could think of was the doctor with whom he registered the family when he first arrived in Nice. Malnutrition and general poor health meant that he had had to consult this man – Doctor Jean Grimaud – fairly often. They had developed a relationship beyond the professional one and had become personal friends. Jean Grimaud lived alone in a small apartment above his surgery on the Promenade des Anglais. Living alone he had come to dine on several evenings with the Asadourians and had many discussions with them, both as to the current situation and the nature of their response.

It had turned out that Grimaud was married and had a Jewish wife. He himself was a Catholic who attended Mass when he could. He had two little girls – Francoise and Denise – who were now thirteen and twelve respectively. All these facts came pouring out of him on an evening when he was told about Hakim's situation and the anxieties that the parents were suffering. It was a long monologue that went on for hours – almost as if he needed a sort of confessional. After living alone for some time, he now craved the confidence of people he could trust. After informing them of the basic facts he went on –

"My wife – Rebecca – was repudiated by her family when she married me. Poor dear, she never got over it. She would visit her mother clandestinely whenever she could. We were living in Paris then and not too far away from her parent's house. But she never again went to the Synagogue. In June 1940, to my shame, we were part of the 'exode' – the great panic-stricken flight from Paris. Were you there by the way?"

"Yes," said Nerissa. "We ourselves didn't budge, but then we were foreigners with proper papers. In fairness, we had less reason to feel the need to move to an area where French government writ might still run. Vahan's decision to stay put was right in the circumstances. Of course we heard about all the experiences so many had suffered when they all filtered back after the armistice."

"In hindsight it was all pretty silly, and I blame myself for having succumbed to the panic," said the Doctor.

"Come, come, many people succumbed in the same way. There is nothing to reproach yourself for."

"Well, maybe, but it was the first of many mistakes I have made during these three years. The panic flight from Paris was a nightmare trip. However, what I possessed, which so many others did not, were some good Michelin road maps. That way I was able to avoid the crowded main roads and could drive down the little-used side roads. I was making for the south. We own a small country house – a little farm really – in the hills not too far from Lyons. These side-roads were almost completely empty, but they had their own different dangers. On the second day out of Paris our car skidded into a ditch. We were in deep countryside and had to traipse across a field to a farmhouse. The farmer was a good man and brought over his two oxen. They pulled us out and we went on our way, but not before paying him well. He in return gave us a big bag of apples and some homemade bread. I can't credit it when I look back on it – both Rebecca and I were petrified – but of what I no longer know. Denise and Francoise on the other hand were having a whale of a time. They loved every minute of it.

That evening, still slipping through villages

and avoiding the towns, we passed a house by the side of the road and saw that the main door was open. We stopped and knocked without getting any answer. We went in and found the house was empty. There was no food, no linen and no clothes. The owners appeared to have completely disappeared. We put some old mattresses on the floor and the girls slept on those. I think that Rebecca and I simply sat up all night. Funny how one's law-abiding habits linger on, even in the face of catastrophe. We left a note of apology with some money when we left the house in the morning."

"Well, did you get to your house near Lyons."

"No. We ran out of petrol in a village near Montlucon. There was a delightful inn there at which we stayed. It served good local food and we lingered there for several days, even though it had not taken me long to find some petrol. We were still there when the Armistice was announced and like so many others we drove back to Paris."

"Do your girls know that their mother is Jewish?"

"Certainly. But of course until recently it hasn't meant much to them. Back in Paris we went through all the same difficulties as everyone else. I was fortunate as I was able to continue my practice. However, it was common knowledge among our neighbours that Rebecca came from an old Jewish family. Eventually she was denounced. The Police – yes of course French police – arrived to insist that both she and the girls should start to wear the yellow star which the Vichy government had decreed. It could have been worse, I suppose.

As a Doctor I still had the use of a car. I carefully saved up my petrol allocation and one day we all left. We were very lucky and again by taking side roads we managed to get across and into the unoccupied zone without being stopped. It was a little easier then. We eventually made it to our home in the village of Montelier. It was very tricky – you know, all the usual difficulty about ration cards and so on. Fortunately the Mayor knew us and we managed to get all our papers confirmed and got our ration books. The farm had some chickens and a goat which had been looked after by a neighbour. I even managed to buy a cow – but frankly, my dear Vahan, I had no idea about country life and my poor Rebecca was even worse. But there was eggs and milk. In the end we needed money and I decided to try and start work again as a Doctor. So I came down here and I send money to Rebecca and the girls whenever I can."

"What made you take that drastic step? Couldn't you find work closer to the family."

"Yes – you may well ask. It all happened in the early part of 1943. Montelier was in the Italian zone. Right next to our little bit of land there was a large Mas in its own grounds that had been taken over by a small Italian garrison. I say garrison but I am referring only to about twenty men and a young officer. I speak a little Italian and this young guy came over to talk to us occasionally. He knew that we were from Paris, and he suspected a Jewish connection though he never said anything. At about the time of the Italian surrender he came across one evening and said – 'Doctor Grimaud.I have some good news and some bad news. The good news is that we are leaving tomorrow. The bad news is that a German unit will be taking over the day after. Perhaps you and your lovely girls should consider leaving.'

"And did you?"

"No. Where could we go. But I myself left the next day. I am still at an age where my presence would be suspicious, so I had to get further away. I am clearly eligible for the Service de Travail Obligatoire to be sent to Germany, and there was a sense that my presence would be a danger to the rest of the family. So I came here and have worked here ever since."

"And the family?"

"Well they are fine. The Germans came, but without any officer. Once Darnand's Milice flooded into the whole area the Germans felt they no longer needed any military presence there and they left. The Mas is empty at the moment. No one knows where the owners have gone. In fact it has turned out for the best. Here I am making some money at what I am trained to do. Meanwhile my three women, without having me to feed, are eating better and get some money from me as well."

This conversation had taken place only a few weeks before the incident at Hakim's school that had precipitated Vahan's decision. Vahan decided that the only contact he could approach whom he could trust was this same Jean Grimaud – but of course it was dangerous if he was wrong about the Doctor. But there really was no one else to whom he could turn. He finally plucked up courage to approach him directly on the matter as they sat together in one of the few cafes still open, facing the sea on the Promenade des Anglais. After explaining his decision and the reasons behind it, he said –

"Look Jean, I'm not looking for heroics. But I have had enough of doing nothing, of taking no part in combating evil. In 1915 and 1916 I did nothing. I simply lay low when it was my own people who were being persecuted – persecuted to their death in most cases. I know there is little I can do, but I have to do something – to help somewhere."

"Vahan – listen - there are two types of Résistants. One like me for the moment … yes, of course I am, your instincts were right … who stays doing their work and living openly, but helping out with funds and information and occasional acts like the hiding of Allied aviators. Then there are the others who live in the deep countryside, fight the Milice and do a lot of sabotage. These are referred to popularly these days as the Maquis."

"Yes I have heard that word bandied about. What does it mean?"

"I'm not too sure but I think it has something to do with Corsican bandits, or the landscape in which they hide. The question is in which group do you see yourself."

There was a long silence. It was one of those moments of decision when a mere straw would have moved his personal destiny one way or another. Grimaud went on –

"The Maquis are certainly better organised now. They even now have recruiting pamphlets, all of which are at pains to stress the difficulties you have to face if you join. Above all, Vahan, it is for the young. It involves an existence hiding in the hills in remote villages, camping out in miserable conditions, sheltering in decrepit abandoned barns or sheds. Above all, you will have to be absolutely cut off from your family."

Grimaud looked at Vahan across the table and then signalled the waiter for another weak and sugarless coffee. Vahan sat staring into space and said nothing. Grimaud stirred his cup, although as there was no sugar it was a fairly meaningless action, and then went on, as if talking to himself –

"They are all improbably young Vahan. I do know of one group who have twice asked me to see to one of their members who had been wounded and needed medical help. When I last went to see them, I had to stay the night. I sat chatting to this young man – no not a man, a mere boy – who had been on guard duty the night before. He talked to me breathlessly about his three-hour watch, about the way he kept thinking that a tree was moving and that it was a German or a milicien."

"So," said Vahan seeming to come out of his reverie and speaking for the first time. "So, Jean, are you being patronising."

"No. This breathless boyish excitement is what being initiated into a Maquis gang feels like for these boys whose fathers are still in prisoner-of-war camps in Germany, and who have had to look at other young men, their occupiers, for years. No, I am not being condescending or superior, but Vahan, it is not for the likes of you and me. We are both over 45 and their boyish enthusiasm is beyond us, isn't it?"

The silence dragged on and then at last Vahan's eyes seemed to focus and he heard himself saying –

"It has to be the Maquis."

In that one moment he had forgotten all his careful, composed and deliberate lifestyle – all that calm application of reason that he had so often over the years pressed on his more emotional and volatile younger brother. In addition he had forgotten the promise he had made to his wife only a few weeks ago. His reply was irrational but it was firm.

"My dear fellow, you do understand that this would mean leaving home, your wife and your son, and all the emotional and physical comforts that go with that. Are you really sure that that is what you want?"

"Yes Jean – I have to do something physically to resist. I've had enough of living in the shadows and accepting wickedness because it is not actually happening to me."

There was something about Vahan's quiet certainty which was enough to fire up Jean Grimaud to a purpose that he had himself been turning over in his own mind for weeks. In a part of his mind he believed that Vahan was only acting out of survivor guilt for events that had occurred almost thirty years ago. But the firmness of his present purpose was clear and with a fire in his own eyes, with his own hand he covered Vahan's lying idly on the table between them, saying-

"Vahan, as I said, I know of a unit of Maquis operating in the countryside just outside Voiron. They have been wanting me to join them for some time as they don't have a doctor. Let's go together. How about it?"

Vahan had not completely lost his normal careful thought processes. He too was fired in return by Jean's enthusiasm, but his mind, now made up, switched back to Nerissa and Hakim.

"What about my family Jean? Do you think that they will be safe here in Nice. Hakim will soon be 13 – it will be difficult for him to stay indoors all the time. If the bloody Milice stop him and strip him as they are doing all the time to other boys, they will see that he is circumcised and…"

Vahan's voice faded out as he began thinking rationally again. It was a very reasonable question which perhaps Vahan should have thought of before he gave such an unequivocal reply to Grimaud's original query. For some time Jean was silent as he considered the problem. In the end his suggestion as to how the matter could be dealt with came out easily, without hesitation or doubts.

"My dear Vahan, the answer is obvious and clears up everything. We take them both to Montelier where they can join Rebecca and my girls. Hakim will even be able to help a bit with the farm-work such as it is. Wonderful! Wonderful. Nerissa will love Rebecca believe me. That's it. Nice is an absolute sink – danger lurks everywhere and you were right to insist on Hakim staying at home – but in the country Hakim can wander around to his heart's content."

It really was the perfect solution. There was no way that either of the men could imagine it was to have such devastating consequences. The atmosphere in Nice was indeed poisonous. More and more schools were being raided, and the number of boys being stopped in the streets being inspected by the vicious Milice was increasing. Every week there would be a few deportees sent to Drancy. From there they would join others from all over France in yet another convoy to Auschwitz.

In the end, it proved easier to persuade Nerissa than Vahan feared. In fact she welcomed the proposal for the family to move to the farm in Montelier. She too was tired of having to live in such a constrained fashion. She felt all the frustrated testosterone of her son cooped up daily in the apartment. But she was not going to give in to Vahan's own decision that easily. She reminded him of his promise. She pointed out that he was nearly fifty and was proposing to join groups comprising young, fit men. She referred to his personal responsibilities and the fact that, after all, he had no reason to fight for the French. Nerissa was clever, she had a command of pure logic superior to most, but she had no way of understanding or coming to terms with the irrational behaviour of others. Vahan felt all the force of her arguments – but he remained sure of his position and eventually Nerissa had to give in.

Early in April 1944, Dr. Grimaud resigned from his practice. Vahan and Nerissa packed their things though they did not give up the apartment, and they all left Nice and arrived at the farmhouse in the village of Montelier.

Chapter 29

The death of Mussolini

By the beginning of 1945 some unity had been achieved in the Italian partisan movement and a chain of command now existed stretching down from General Cadorna, who had been accepted as overall commander by the bulk of the Partisan movement.

The war was coming to its climax and in North Italy, as the Germans were retreating, they were being continually harassed by Cadorna's partisans. As each day passed, a whole series of arrangements were under constant discussion between Cadorna, Schuster the Cardinal Bishop of Milan, and General Wolff the German commander of the SS troops still in the area, all designed to try and minimize the destruction normally attendant on a retreating army.

Nicolai and Count Pietro Bellini had managed to keep together throughout most of their time with the partisans during the previous year. Now as the months passed and the war began to lurch to its 'Gotterdammerung' ending, they again found themselves stationed together. They were with a partisan group in the hills at the north end of Lake Como above a village on the lakeside called Dongo. Bellini was the officer in charge

Peering through binoculars, Nicolai, who was on sentry duty that morning, called out –

"Pietro, there is a convoy of lorries together with three armoured cars, winding its way north on the coast road. They are already within range. It looks to me as if there are about 150 SS soldiers. I can't see any machine guns."

"Keep a lookout – I've already sent Luigi and his group down to have that tree dragged across the road just after Dongo. They are down there at the moment, I can see them, filling it all out with rocks."

"Hey! They appear to have stopped," called out Nicolai. Pietro swung round and trained his own binoculars on the lakeside road below.

"Let's show them we are here. Open fire everyone at will," he called out.

Shots rang out rather raggedly from their positions. They did not seem to be doing much damage, but then neither was the return fire from the now stationary vehicles on the lakeside road below. The shooting died out on both sides and Pietro called out –

"OK – cease fire! Come on Nicolai – and you too Lieutenant Stelle – lets see what we have here."

"Holding up a white flag the three officers clambered down the hillside towards the stationary convoy. As they approached, the German officer in charge of the convoy came forward to meet them before they could cross the road. He introduced himself as Lieutenant Hans Fallmeyer. He spoke Italian fluently –

"Gentlemen – I have orders to take my troops

further up the valley and from there to go through the Pass and back into Germany to continue the fight against the Anglo-Saxons. Look we have no intention of fighting Italians and I believe that there is a general withdrawal of all German forces in North Italy already proceeding. You will find, Captain, that there is currently an agreement brokered by Cardinal Schuster between the German High Command and your General Cadorna allowing German troops to retire unhindered in order to avoid the destruction of North Italian cities."

"I have not received any such orders yet, Lieutenant – though I have heard rumours of meetings taking place with a view to facilitate the retreat. But I must warn you, I have mortars and a machine gun up there in the hills above us, commanding this whole road, and I have constructed a road block a little further down the road."

Nicolai glanced in amazement at his friend, knowing that all they had between the whole group were rifles and a dozen grenades. They could not have stood up against these German regulars for a moment in the event of a serious fire fight breaking out.

There now arose a temporary stand-off as Fallmeyer returned to the convoy to confer with his two Sergeants, while Nicolai, Pietro and Stelle drew off to consider their own options.

Unbeknown to the three Partisan officers, the convoy in fact included several of the leading ministers in the government of the North Italian

Fascist state. But even more dramatically, in the lead armoured car was Mussolini himself. To this day it is really impossible to declare for certain what exactly Mussolini intended when he joined this group going up the beautiful lakeside road along the Lago di Como. Did he mean to go to Switzerland – to Germany – to a last ditch suicidal battle in the Valtellina? Who knows? It was probably pure lethargy and a desire to get it all over. Whatever the motivation, there he was waiting to move on with the German troops.

The Partisan officers conferred –

"Look Stelle have you heard anything about these arrangements?"

"Yes, Captain, to be honest I have heard rumours. In return for German undertakings not to carry out any destruction of buildings, bridges and industries, our Partisan commander is proposing to allow the Germans to retire unhindered. But there is no question of letting any Italians go with them – voluntarily or otherwise."

"Is an agreement actually in force?"

"I have no idea, Captain"

"Look – I'll have to go and find out. It sounds all right, but we've got to be sure. I'll get Fallmeyer to drive us both back down the road and I will try telephoning Milan to see if I can get some orders. Meanwhile Nicolai you remain here and try to make sure the convoy stays put."

Fallmeyer agreed to go with Bellini, and in the hot midday sun the stalemate continued. Meanwhile sitting with Mussolini in the front armoured car was Claretta Petacci – the Duce's mistress. Despite every effort made by Donna Rachele, Mussolini's wife, she had been outwitted by this girl, who had managed to remain with her lover till the end.

When Fallmeyer and Count Bellini returned it had been agreed that the Germans were to be allowed to proceed, but that any Italians with the party would be handed over to the partisans. The convoy could move on down the road but would have to stop in Dongo to be searched. Fallmeyer indicated that he would have to confer with his men. He moved to the convoy to discuss the situation further. In effect, what he needed to decide was what was to be done about Mussolini. Fallmeyer conferred with the demoralised man and urged on by Claretta, Mussolini donned a German military overcoat and hid with the German troops in the first of the lorries. Fallmeyer had no intention of saving any of the Fascist ministers in the lorries further down the line and Mussolini knew this.

The convoy started up and moved on to Dongo where it stopped in front of the town hall. There the partisans began searching the lorries and looking into the armoured cars. The Fascist ministers were all dragged out and locked up in the town hall. Claretta was not recognised but was taken out and left at the side of the road as she was clearly an Italian civilian.

However much Mussolini may have been a somewhat tragic figure, and however much he can be praised for holding out against some of Hitler's demonic requirements about the Italian Jews, what was now occurring was a final betrayal on his part. He had refused to flee abroad earlier, making it impossible for any of his followers to do so, but now he was abandoning them to their fate in order to save his own skin. For what? To die in Germany instead of Italy! By this point he was simply not thinking straight.

As the search continued and the Fascist ministers were led away, the moment inevitably came when Mussolini was recognised. The Germans were now indifferent – their only desire was to get away as soon as they could. Shouting and excitement grew as the news went round the watching crowds that it was Mussolini – Mussolini himself – who had been taken. Nicolai and Pietro arrived just as Mussolini was clambering out of the lorry guarded by one of the partisans – Giovanni Lazzaro – who had been the one who had recognised him. Pietro said –

"What's going on Lazzaro?"

"Look – look – the man who made the world quake, the man who excited me so much when I was a kid and who I came to hate is there – there!"

"Does he have any weapons?"

"No, no, he has already handed his pistol over to me."

At about this moment in the hurried exchange there was some angry shouting and murmuring from the crowd on the other side of the road. Count Pietro turned to Mussolini who was looking apprehensive and said –

"Don't worry! While you remain here in our charge not a hair of your head will be touched."

Nicolai gave a sort of strangled gasp as he tried to suppress the almost hysterical laughter that was forcing itself up from his insides as he considered the indubitable fact that Bellini had chosen the wrong expression, was in fact referring to a man without a single hair on his head. Mussolini never uttered a word – just staring ahead in a kind of dazed lethargy, a mood which never left him.

It took a bit more time for the situation to be sorted out in Dongo. The Fascist ministers remained for the moment locked up in the town hall, while Mussolini was taken by Pietro and Nicolai with the rest of the partisans to a house further up the hillside which had a telephone. Meanwhile, the German troops moved on out of Italy and out of history.

The news of Mussolini's arrest, phoned through to Cadorna's headquarters, was relayed to all the allied commanders within an hour. They immediately began badgering Cadorna, each demanding that he should be handed over to them. Meanwhile back at Dongo, Mussolini asked Bellini to find out what had happened to Claretta. Pietro sent Nicolai down to find her and give her the message that Mussolini was close by and under arrest. The girl was in tears and still standing outside the town hall. She prevailed on Nicolai to take her back with him, as she wanted to be with her lover. Nicolai did so and Mussolini and Claretta were reunited.

At one o'clock the following morning the two cars commandeered by Bellini set off driving south towards Milan in the dark. In the cars, as well as the three officers and two of the partisans were Mussolini and Claretta. Blustering their way through the road blocks with a mixture of authority and natural aristocratic arrogance, they eventually reached their destination. This was a house belonging to the parents of one of the partisans – a villa at 8 Via Del Riale – another building in the hills above the Lake. There was no direct road to it. The whole party had to climb up a mule track to get there. It was pouring with rain and pitch black. Poor Claretta had only high heel shoes and was exhausted. Nicolai and Pietro held her up on either side as they struggled up the path.

Mussolini and Claretta spent their last night together in the main bedroom belonging to these simple people, while Nicolai, Stelle, Bellini and the two others sat up and talked all the rest of the night about what they now proposed to do. Early the next morning with first light, Nicolai was sent in one of the cars to report directly to General Cadorna in Milan. As a result, he was not present as the drama unfolded at the villa.

The Anglo-American Allies had now occupied Milan and even had advance units in the town of Como, not all that far from where Mussolini was being held. In the discussions going on amongst all the Italian groups involved, the one thing on which every spectrum of opinion agreed – from the Monarchists to the Communists – was that Mussolini was not to be handed over to the Allies. A public trial of Mussolini would be a trial of Fascist Italy and no party wanted that. Death would be the eventual result in either case, but that death should be carried out by Italians, not by foreigners.

Early that morning before Nicolai had arrived, the Central Committee in Milan despatched one of their officers, with orders to see what was going on. No one ever acknowledged what further secret orders he may have been given. The officer sent was Walter Audisio, who was a member of the PCI. He was known for his ruthless decisiveness. It has never been clear whether he was sent in the knowledge that it was likely that he would arrange the executions that everyone wanted. On his arrival at the hillside villa, he confronted Bellini and demanded a list of all the prisoners that had been taken in Dongo the day before. Taking the list he marked against each name a tick or the word 'death'. Pietro objected and wanted to know why there was to be no trial or tribunal. Audisio shouted back at him the one word –

"Hypocrisy!"

Pietro looked again at the list and saw the word 'death' against the name Petacci. He again remonstrated saying –

"Petacci – Clara Petacci – but why, why? You want to shoot a woman. She's not guilty of anything except loving the wrong man."

"Nonsense man she is as guilty as the rest of them."

Count Bellini continued to object, but at that point Audisio pulled out his revolver, his face white with rage, and ordered Bellini to get out. The situation was fluid – Audisio appeared to have the authority, but if Nicolai had been there, and if they had been backed up by Stelle, who as it happened was also away, things might have turned out differently. The two other partisans would have followed their own officers, and with their support and those of Nicolai and Stelle, Audisio might have been forcibly overruled. But Pietro was alone and he had to give way.

Mussolini was taken out and shot there and then. Neither of the three original partisan officers were present and there were something like twenty different accounts of who did what by the stone wall outside the house. Whether the pathetic Claretta threw herself in front of Mussolini, as was reported in some accounts, or whether she was separately gunned down was never cleared up in the investigations that followed. But what was completely clear was the shameful final act. The bodies of Mussolini and Claretta, together with a couple of fascist ministers were piled into the back of a lorry to Milan and dumped in the Piazzale Loreto. It was still the early morning. People gathered and began abusing the dead bodies – particularly those of Mussolini and Claretta. Young men arrived and kicked the corpses repeatedly. Somebody stuck a flag between the fingers of the dead man's hand. The crowd grew and grew and the desecration got worse. The scene became medieval in a macabre way, like a painting by Hieronymous Bosch.

Meanwhile, Nicolai had been told to report directly to General Cadorna and his appointment was for 11.00 a.m. He was told that he would have to explain exactly what had happened at Dongo and where Mussolini was currently being kept. He was walking in the Piazza San Babila on his way, though it was still early, when crowds ran past him shouting – 'They have taken him – they have taken him – he's in the Piazzale Loreto.' Nicolai followed the crowd. When he arrived in the square he could not believe what he saw as he was pushed to the front. Mussolini's jaw was broken and his skull cracked. One of his eyes appeared to have been gouged out. A woman had urinated on his body and another had produced a revolver and was firing it into the body as Nicolai stood and watched.

The crowd was getting hysterical and the few partisans who had been deputed to guard the bodies were becoming nervous. People at the back of the crowd started yelling that they could not see and demanded that the bodies should be strung up so everyone could see. People were shouting and cursing as Nicolai slowly backed out and turned away from the gruesome sight. His last view as he hurried away for his interview was of the corpses of Mussolini and Claretta being hauled up – hanging upside down – Claretta's skirt fell over her face revealing her underwear. Amid the jeers and catcalls of the crowd one of the Partisans stretched up, raised her skirt and tucked it between her legs in order to try and retain some sense of decency.

Nicolai ran to his rendezvous with Cadorna, not because he was late, but because he was distressed. For once his normally cool and reserved nature, instilled into him by his English governess, deserted him. As he was led, or rather burst into Cadorna's office, he gave a perfunctory salute and began bitterly complaining about what was going on at the Piazzale Loreto –

"Sir you simply cannot allow it – it is shameful – shameful.

There can be no excuse, no excuse at all, regardless of what people may have suffered."

"My dear Lieutenant, for God's sake calm down – what is the matter with you?"

Nicolai began describing what was going on – but Cadorna waved him to silence and said –

"Listen Lieutenant and listen carefully as I will not repeat myself. I have already been told what is happening by Cardinal Schuster. He was even more excited than you, warning me that if I didn't arrange to have the bodies taken down, he would go personally to the Piazzale and do it himself. So the matter is right now being dealt with. You are right – it is shameful, of course it is, and the whole insurrection and the Partisan movement has been dishonoured as a result. But this is history in the making. No one can endorse desecration of the dead – but it is necessary that people see and understand that justice has been done and that an era has passed. We need this chapter in our nation's history to be closed – and shameful though it might now appear – it has now been effectively closed."

Nicolai, whose natural calm and diffidence had already re-surfaced said nothing. Then, seeing that obviously there was no need for him to remain and report, he saluted, but then said before leaving –

"And the woman – the girl – was her death and bodily degradation also necessary for a chapter in your nation's history to be satisfactorily closed."

Cadorna looked hard at him but said nothing more.

Chapter 30

Frenchman v Frenchman

Doctor Grimaud had been right. Rebecca and Nerissa had got on together right from the start. At the same time the three children, a little shy at first, soon became great friends. Francoise and Denise had never played with or enjoyed the company of boys. In Paris they had gone to an all-girls school. In Montelier, while the local school was indeed mixed, there were not many boys of their age. In fact throughout occupied France there was an extraordinary inbalance of the sexes. Two million young men were still either prisoners of war in Germany or were caught up in the STO and were in forced labour camps. Then on top of that it was dangerous for other young men and for boys of over 14 to be seen in the streets, so they too were either in hiding or had joined the Maquis.

Both the Germans in the north and the Vichy Milice in the south were regularly checking out boys once they reached the age of puberty or looked as if they might be eligible for the STO to be sent to Germany to work, In these circumstances and certainly after they reached the age of 14, the local farmers kept their sons on the farm and away from the prying eyes of the Milice.

Vahan and Jean only stayed a couple of days before leaving to join a Maquis unit living rough in the Voiron district. Once contacted, Jean, already known to the leader was welcomed enthusiastically. The group, ranging from diehard communists on the one hand to lapsed and disillusioned Petainists on the other, looked a bit askance at Vahan. Grimaud however made it clear that it was a package deal – accepting him meant also accepting Vahan. Soon, Vahan, despite the foreign accent, was a full and trusted member of the group.

The terrible events of Glieres had come and gone. The Voiron group, now led by a Colonel from the old regular army, were not likely to fall into the trap of facing up to regular German troops as had happened at Glieres. But full-scale civil war had broken out between the Milice and the Maquis, though in most places it was not clear who was the hunter and who the hunted. To begin with, when Darnand first took over throughout the south, there was little doubt. The Milice had military equipment provided by the Vichy government, and the general public had not as yet turned against them. But by the spring of 1944, when Vahan and Jean joined, the Maquisards were getting more confident. It was increasingly obvious that the Germans were going to lose the war. More and more equipment in the form of rifles and machine guns were dropped by the Allied air forces into the hands of the Maquis. As a result, more reprisal attacks were made on Milice barracks and on those Vichy officials who were held to be acting oppressively against the local population.

Then in June 1944, the Allies landed in Normandy and the whole situation changed again.
There were now three battles going on in France.
There was the battle between the German army
and the Allies in the north; there was a slow-burn-
ing battle between Germans and local French Résistants throughout France; and finally there was
an increasingly violent and passionate battle between French and French – between the Maquis
and the Milice.

The Milice Francaise had come into existence
early in 1943. Led by the extreme right-wing
Darnand, it adopted a uniform of dark blue jackets. It's marching song included the words – "For
those who brought about our defeat – no punishment is hard enough.". The oath of allegiance it
demanded from its supporters contained all the
usual right-wing litany, directed against all the
usual targets. It ended – "I swear to fight against
democracy, against Gaullist insurrection and
against the Jewish leprosy."

The Vichy government, not allowed any functioning army by the terms of the armistice, came
to rely on the Militia to counter the threat from
what they regarded as the lawless terrorists of
the Maquis. In a way, the Maquis and the Milice
were two sides of the same coin They each relied
for their existence on the existence of the other.
Hatred developed. So far as the resistance was
concerned, the Miliciens were not like the Wehrmacht soldiers – simply German conscripts doing
their duty. In the eyes of the Maquisards, they

were French volunteers betraying their country. For the Milice, on the other hand, the Resistance fighters were simply lawless thieves and outlaws fighting against their legitimate government, determined to destabilise the country for their own ends. One of the best-known broadcasters of the time – Philipe Henriot – used all his power of journalistic articulation over the radio to applaud the Milice as guardians of law and order.

As the year wore on, hate figures on both sides were murdered. Georges Mandel, a former member of Blum's government and in Reynaud's last cabinet, who had tried to stand firm in opposing the armistice, and who wished to stick by the British alliance, was murdered. He was collected from prison by some Miliciens, pretending to be police, taken to the forest of Fontainebleu, thrown out of the car and shot. This resulted in Henriot then being kidnapped and shot. Henriot was given a state funeral conducted at Notre Dame cathedral in Paris, officiated by Monsignor Suchard – the Cardinal-Archbishop of Paris. More hatred and more passion was generated by each succeeding murder.

Vahan had already gone on several missions with his group – at first just tagging along as Jean's assistant. By dint of his aptitude for learning, and due to the care and attention that he gave to detail, he had become a master of the technique of the delayed-fuse bomb or grenade. This had become a very useful accomplishment, and the group had blown up railway lines in and

out of Lyons on several occasions. A few weeks
before the Allies landed, the group had been required to make a raid directly into Voiron itself,
with a view to assassinating the particularly obnoxious chief of the Milice operating in the area.

This was a man whose hands were stained with
the blood of many young men and boys. He was
known to have tortured and killed men who had
no connection with the Resistance and without
due process of law. He had a vicious whip with
which he was known to beat prisoners – particularly adolescent boys – to death. He was known
to be staying at his home in Voiron when Vahan's
group struck. The operation was faultlessly executed and according to plan. The group led by
their Colonel – Texier – quietly surrounded the
house at night and then stormed in and captured
it without a shot being fired. Grimaud was not
with them, but Vahan had been brought along
to deal with the demolition. The house was to be
blown up as a warning after they had executed
the Milice chief and withdrawn.

However, in the house with the Milice chief
and two bodyguards, both of whom were killed
with a knife as the party first stormed in, was the
man's wife and three small children. The family of five were gathered together in the parent's
bedroom. Vahan was ordered to go and set his
bombs and fuses in the rest of the building.

As he finished his task and set all the fuses for
fifteen minutes he heard several shots and assumed that it had taken that many to finish off

the Milice chief. He and the young man helping him finished the job and then Vahan ran upstairs calling out –

"All the fuses are set. It's going to blow in fifteen minutes. We've got to go. Quick – for god's sake move yourselves and get the woman and kids out of the house."

He burst into the bedroom and stopped in his tracks. The local Head of the Milice was there still alive standing in the middle of the room – his face white and with vomit all over himself. Dotted around the room on the bed and on the floor were the bodies of the three children and their mother, all dead and with their blood still flowing. The six Maquisards and Colonel Texier stood silently, staring at the retching man. There was a final moment of silence as Vahan burst in, then Texier raised his pistol and with one shot put the man out of his misery. Vahan might have been sick himself if he had had a moment to think – but he had to get everyone out first. He shouted again, though this time his voice came out in a strangled squeak –

"Everyone out, everyone out – it's going to blow in ten minutes."

When they all got back to the remote farmhouse in the hills which was their headquarters, Vahan tackled Texier about the shooting of the wife and children. He was not going to be browbeaten and the two men shouted at each other. In the end, Vahan saw that there was nothing more to say and he turned to leave the room. But at the door he turned and said before leaving –

"Very well, I may understand your arguments, but the woman – the mother – and above all the three little children – were their deaths also necessary in order to make the message clear?"

Texier looked hard at him as he left but said nothing more.

Chapter 31

The last deportations

Meanwhile life in the little farm in Montelier went on fairly cheerfully. Before leaving, Vahan had given orders that Hakim was not to go to the local school with the girls. He was to spend two hours every morning with Nerissa doing school-work, then, in the rest of the day, he was to work on the farm under Rebecca's direction. Once Francoise and Denise were back they could all play together if Hakim had finished all the chores he had been given.

The girls, who, prior to Hakim's arrival, had dawdled on their way back from school, now hurried home. They looked forward to the make-believe games that Hakim made up. The two mothers, anxious, and with more urgent problems to think about, made no attempt to supervise the children. Central European Time, enforced by the Germans throughout France, meant that while the mornings were dark, the evenings were very light and dragged on. Make-believe was all very well, up to a point, but all three children were on the verge of puberty. Francoise was almost nubile. She and Denise had already been talking together about their burgeoning sexuality for the last few months.

Hakim was shyer, but he was thirteen and was already suffering – if that is the right word – embarrassing erections and night-time emissions. In normal circumstances, both Vahan and Nerissa would have talked with him and given whatever reassurance was necessary. But these were not normal times. In Nice, Vahan had thought to himself that it was time he had a talk with his son, but had then left before he had had the chance. Nerissa, meanwhile, was far too preoccupied with helping to get everyone enough to eat, without having to cope with the problems of male adolescence.

Hakim's lively imagination did not, as it happens extend to his own developing sexuality. He was fairly naïve and without the stimulation of prurient discussions with his school-friends, his sexual knowledge was rather neglected. He enjoyed the company of the two girls, but he had not consciously indulged in any sexual fantasies in which they figured. The opposite, however, was not the case. While Denise had simply become very curious about 'boys', Francoise quite definitely found that she was having sexual fantasies for the first time in her life with respect to a particular boy.

So it was that make-believe began to go a little further. It was all fairly innocent. They tried a little kissing together though it did not get very far. It came to a head one day when the girls – it was Denise actually who made the running – said to Hakim –

"You're Jewish aren't you?"

"Yes I am," replied Hakim, who knew perfectly

well that the girls were themselves half Jewish.

"Well, we keep being told about Jewish boys being circumcised. What does that exactly mean?"

Hakim blushed and at first tried to avoid answering. But their experimentation had gone too far for him to get out of it and eventually he tried to explain. Francoise, who had seen other little boys, understood what circumcision meant, although all she really knew was that a cut of some sort on the boy's penis was involved. However she kept the knowledge to herself and pretended not to know anything either. Denise had no idea at all and demanded a practical demonstration. Eventually after days of avoidance, Hakim finally agreed to show them in the privacy and dark of the old barn. Francoise took one look and then blushed deeply at her own reaction and turned away. But Denise had no such shyness and stared and stared and wouldn't let Hakim pull up his trousers for several minutes.

That was it. It never went further than that. Denise never thought of asking again, whilst Francoise, who might well have liked to, did not dare.

It was in late June with the Allies still stuck in Normandy unable to break out, when fate struck. No one ever knew who, out of the nine hundred inhabitants of the little village of Montelier, wrote the anonymous letter of denunciation. But someone certainly did, as after the war the letter, amongst many others, was found in the files of the Lyons municipal authority. It read –

"Whilst not wishing to expose anyone to danger I would draw your attention to the fact that living with Madame Grimaud and her two innocent and vulnerable daughters are two refugees from Paris – a mother and her son who does not go to school and is almost certainly over 15. They are surely Jewish refugees, and I think that they should be investigated before they corrupt French minors."

Within two days of receiving this letter, a small detachment of Vichy Milice, led by a dedicated Darnand supporter, arrived at the farm one afternoon in their sleek black Citroen. It was a grey and cheerless afternoon, a change from the glorious summer days experienced up to then. The whole family were in the big farmhouse living-room when the car drew up. The three young Milice strode into the room through the main door, without knocking and with drawn revolvers in their hands. Everyone had by then risen from their seats and remained standing, looking with alarm at the three young men. It was all fairly undramatic and seemed to be over in a surprisingly short time. There was no heroics or displays of emotion. It was immediately clear that they had been well briefed as their questions were directed straight at Nerissa and Hakim who happened to be standing together.

"Your name and papers," snapped the young Lieutenant.

Nerissa went to the desk in the corner of the room and took out some papers saying –

"My name is Nerissa Asadourian and this is my

son."

"Ah – I see his name is Hakim Benussan – that is a Jewish name is it not?"

"No, no – Turkish. We are Turkish citizens – see."

There was a short silence as the officer scrutinised the passports.

"And where Madame are your individual identity papers?" This was greeted by silence as Nerissa tried to think fast. Then he pointed at Hakim and said –

"Take down your trousers, boy."

Hakim did not know what to do. He looked at his mother – but Nerissa too was in a state of shock and stood silent giving him no support. He fumbled to undo his buttons, but still his trousers remained up. The young French Lieutenant nodded to his two henchmen, who levelled their guns at the two women. He then strode forward and with one vicious gesture he tore down the trousers and then Hakim's underpants.

There was a long and pregnant silence as all eyes inevitably turned towards the poor boy's circumcised member.

"You are under arrest Madame," said the Lieutenant.

"But why – why – we've done nothing," shouted Nerissa, suddenly coming back to life.

"Madame Grimaud," said the young man ignoring Nerissa's outburst, "you may go and collect what few things these two may need for the next few days – in one small suitcase only. Furthermore you should be aware that you yourself may be in trouble for harbouring undesirable elements."

Rebecca was just about to reply – a defiant protest that exposed something about her own position perhaps – but Nerissa sensing that she might say something which could compromise her and the two girls as well, said quickly –

"Rebecca, please collect my things for a 3 or 4 day stay away and a change of clothes for Hakim as well. That small suitcase at the top of the stairs should do it. Please go. Thank you."

Hakim had by now pulled up his trousers. The young Lieutenant motioned them out. Hakim smiled diffidently and with a shy warmth at the two girls, who were both staring at him with round frightened eyes, and walked out behind Nerissa. They were made to sit in the back of the Citroen squeezed in between the two Milice men. The Lieutenant came out carrying the little suitcase and got into the front seat next to the driver with the suitcase on his lap.

Rebecca was now openly weeping and holding on tightly to Francoise and Denise. The two girls were frightened but they were not crying. They were of course unaware of the danger. They all stood at the door and watched as the car sped away. No one waved.

The Voiron Maquis group, led by Colonel Texier and with Vahan as their explosives expert, were well aware that even at this late stage in the war, convoys were still setting out from Lyons carrying arrested Jews and captured Résistants to the internment camp at Drancy. On two occasions, they managed to sabotage the rail line which ran from Lyons to Paris. This had the effect of delaying some trains, but their explosives were simply not powerful enough to cause really extensive damage. When they blew up a section of the line it would rarely take more than 48 hours for it to be repaired. On several occasions it was suggested that they should wait for the arrival of one of the deportation trains and blow it up as it passed. But then they might risk injuring the passengers in the cattle trucks. It was a dilemma and it was never entirely resolved.

Meanwhile the Allies were about to break out of Normandy. The total liberation of France was likely to be only weeks away. Now the Allied High Command became more and more interested in attempts by the Resistance to disrupt rail transport throughout France. Already several Panzer Divisions stationed in the south had been badly delayed in getting to Normandy by a combination of Allied airpower during the day, and the Maquis activity blowing up railway lines during the night. High explosives were dropped into the hands of the better known and more effective Maquis groups – and one of those was Colonel Texier's men.

Vahan, as the group's explosive expert, immediately used some of these explosives to blow up a section of the line from Grenoble to Lyons just ahead of a train carrying an Infantry regiment northwards. He intended to blow up the engine as it passed over, thus causing the most damage and probably killing many of the soldiers, but he found that it was very difficult to be precisely accurate about when the fuse would blow and in this instance it went off too soon. Nevertheless it had an enormous effect and caused a huge explosion and a great crater into which the train ploughed. The men with him – not one of whom was over twenty – were exhilarated by the night's expedition, and when they got back they persuaded Texier to let them try again – but this time on the main Lyons – Paris line.

When Nerissa and Hakim arrived at the Milice headquarters in Lyons they were immediately separated and imprisoned. Nerissa was interviewed the next morning – and was interviewed on several days following – always by different men. The situation in the Milice headquarters in Lyons was Kafkaesque. No one listened to Nerissa's complaints, neither her continual assertions that she was a legitimate Turkish citizen, nor that Hakim was her natural son. Moslems also circumcised their boys she kept repeating over and over again. Unfortunately, when interrogated she was quite unable to establish to anyone's satisfaction that she was herself a Moslem. She had of course carefully made sure that when she had been asked to present her papers back at the farm that she should not take out Hakim's nufus, with the tell-tale 'Yahudi' on it, out of the desk drawer. However the visa for the family stamped in her passport clearly gave the name of her son as Hakim Benussan. For most of the Milice, any name beginning 'Ben' automatically meant it was Jewish.

She found that despite all her intelligence, and despite spending all night thinking of what to say next, she was contradicting herself all the time. She had had the presence of mind to bring with her only her own nufus and not Hakim's, but this clearly stated 'Ermeni', and even the uneducated Milice men were fully aware that if you were 'Ermeni' you could not be Moslem. The conditions at the offices of the Lyons Milice were in any case chaotic as the Vichy government began to totter to its end. The whole state apparatus was crumbling. Any semblance of law and order was breaking down. Yet the more chaotic the situation became, the more frantic was the reaction of the Milice officers.

It was about two weeks before the liberation of Paris that it was decided that Nerissa and Hakim were to be put onto the next train heading for Paris and Drancy. They would be joining a group of another forty men and some women and children. This party included a group of nine young Résistants who had been captured a few days before, together with several Jewish families, including children, who had fallen into the Milice net.

Nerissa, traumatised and afraid, without any certain knowledge of where she and Hakim were being sent, never lost her innate ability to analyse and think logically. She realised that she had made a mess of the interrogations. Her attempt to portray Hakim as a pure Turk – a practising Moslem – had probably been her best way out. But she had then tripped up by trying to suggest that he was her natural son. She was nevertheless quite clear in her own mind that she would not under any circumstances abandon him. Clinging together and comforting each other, they stood and swayed about in the cattle truck which was about to set off to Drancy.

News that the nine young Résistants captured by the Milice were to be loaded onto a train leaving for Drancy arrived at Texier's headquarters twenty-four hours before the train was due to leave. The Voiron Maquis group had a clandestine radio contact with a young supporter – Jean-Pierre – who lived in Lyons in a shabby apartment overlooking the main station. He kept an eye on everything the Germans were doing and all the movements in and out of the main station. He was also able, with some help, to keep a watch on the activities of the local Milice. It was he who had forewarned the Voiron group, and agreed to keep radio contact open to monitor the arrival of the nine Résistants and the time of departure of the train.

There was no hesitation this time in the Texier group. Most of the recently dropped high explosive was still available, and this time Vahan decided that he would take the risk of setting off the explosive himself, rather than relying on a delayed fuse. It would have to be done very carefully if the truck carrying the prisoners was not to be badly damaged. Texier agreed that a proper detachment of experienced armed men should go with Vahan in order to save the prisoners and combat the inevitable troops guarding the train.

They had a full 24 hours to get into position north of Lyons at a spot where there was an incline and where the train would be going slowly. Radio contact with Jean-Pierre was maintained as the group made its way to the ambush spot. Texier himself had decided to come at the last moment. They travelled separately in a wide variety of wheels. Vahan and the explosives, together with Texier and the Radio man went in a car – ramshackle and battered but still serviceable. Crossing the Rhone as they went north was the most dangerous moment, but all went well. The bridge chosen was manned by the police and not the Milice

Everyone was in place at least an hour before the convoy to Drancy was due to set off. Vahan was more nervous than he had been in previous expeditions. He had heard from Jean-Pierre that there were some Jewish families also on the train in the same truck as the Résistants. A mere few seconds error in pressing the plunger might make all the difference between blowing up the engine or blowing up the truck carrying the prisoners. But all was ready as the group waited to hear from Jean-Pierre that the train had set off.

Then the message arrived. The men waited tensely for the news and it was mostly good. The train had just left. A flat railcar had been added on which stood German guards manning machine guns behind a sand-bagged emplacement – but it had been attached immediately behind the engine. This meant that when the engine blew up, the chances were that the guards would be blown up too – leaving only a few guards on the roof of one of the carriages at the rear. However, the cattle truck containing the prisoners was immediately behind the flat-car with the machine gun post, and so again any error would be fatal. Vahan was seriously concerned as he checked and rechecked his wiring as they all waited.

There was only about twenty minutes to go when there was an excited call from Jean-Pierre. Leaving only ten minutes after the deportation train, was another train carrying forty tanks for the SS Panzer Das Reich division, heading north to join the defensive line north of Paris. An urgent call had come from the Allied liaison officer emphasising the importance of dealing as a matter of urgency with this train if possible. There was a hurried consultation amongst the group.

They had all been buoyed up to arrange the rescue of their nine comrades. But, in the end, Texier made the decision supported by Vahan. The nine Résistants were fighters. They might even escape – they were soldiers who had volunteered. They could not use their precious explosives to save them. The tanks had to be destroyed.

Vahan was relieved – he was no longer nervous – the Tank-conveyor train was an easier target and the deaths of the prisoners in the event of an error would not be on his conscience. The whole group watched silently as the deportation train went slowly by. Ten minutes later with an enormous roar the tank train followed and was blown up to a great cheer by all the young men, as rifle fire broke out from those guards still left alive – and was enthusiastically returned. There were forty tanks less for the bitter defensive battle raging in the north. Every member of the Voiron group got back safely.

It was only ten days before the liberation of Paris that the penultimate deportation convoy left Drancy for Auschwitz. It was the 66th departure, and on it, still clinging together, both weak from hunger and lack of good drinking water, were Nerissa and Hakim Asadourian.

Like so many others, they were never heard of again.

The last – the 67th – convoy left Drancy for Auschwitz a few days later on the 17th August

1944.

Within only a few weeks the whole of France was liberated, and less than a year later the war in Europe came to an end.

Chapter 32

Vahan

Vahan had been completely shattered, his mind broken, by the deportation and death of Hakim and Nerissa. He had not heard anything until he and his friend Dr. Grimaud returned to visit their wives soon after the liberation of the whole of France, and Rebecca Grimaud told the terrible story. Despite all the support that the Grimauds tried to give him, he was unable to face up to the facts. He could not rid himself of that most difficult of all guilts – the guilt of the survivor. He had first felt it, though not to the same extent, at the moment when he heard of the death of his mother and all his sisters during the deportations of 1915-16 in Turkey. At that time he was still young and a good deal more resilient. He had felt it again after the death of his brother and after reading his letter.

Guilt now struck him with a force he could not cope with. Why had he survived and not they? It was he who had put himself deliberately into danger – should he not have stayed at home in order to protect his family? His mind went round and round, dwelling on the facts of the way he had dealt with his family's well-being from the moment of the Fall of France. The more he thought, the more he saw all his actions as mistake after mistake. The more he considered the events of the past three years and the decisions he had arrived at, the more his mind rejected everything he had tried to do. Sometimes he would wake up in the night in a complete sweat, screaming at his thoughts spiralling out of control

– Right from the very start he should have been more aware about the possible danger to Hakim. Then there was the move away from Paris – had that really been necessary? The conditions in Nice after the surrender of Italy had in many ways been worse than in Paris. Then abandoning his family – for that is what it amounted to didn't it – how could he? Leaving them in that bloody village!--

Usually by that point Vahan would be exhausted and go back to bed. His health deteriorated and he took no part in the celebrations which marked the end of the war in Europe. Vahan, born at the end of the nineteenth century, was a creature of that halcyon period before 1914 when humane liberalism was at its height. He was 18 when war broke out, but he had already taken in and fully accepted the philosophy of the 'Principia Ethica'. What mattered in life is one's state of mind, and this has little to do with your actions, malevolent or benevolent. The ultimate values in life, for Vahan, were 'love' and 'beauty'. These were to be found principally in the enjoyment of personal relationships of all kinds, coupled to the appreciation of art. Above all Vahan developed a belief in a free mind and the ultimate virtue of the human race. Human beings in this philosophy are basically 'good' and 'moral' until they are corrupted by institutions – religious or national.

All this was shaken by the events of 1915 and the deaths of hundreds of thousands of his own people at the hands of the Ottoman state in the deportations of that year. But in the end the belief was shaken not shattered. He bounced back. He was in love and he had married. He adopted a son whom he loved. He went to live in Paris, one of the most civilised and cultured cities in the world. There, he could continue to believe that while there are terrible brutalities in the world, the virtue of the human individual will always triumph in the end. He, too, believed passionately in the well-known aphorism, to which he added religion, and re-stated in his own way –

"I hate the idea of 'causes', particularly nationalist and religious ones. If I was obliged to choose between betraying my country and religion on the one hand or betraying my friend and neighbour on the other, I hope that I would have the moral strength to betray my country."

So to a man like Vahan – the ultimate betrayal, the betrayal that condemned his son and his wife to a terrifying ordeal and eventual death, caused a total collapse in his psyche. Finally, after the war fully ended and the world drifted at last into 1946, Vahan's state became such that Dr. Grimaud placed him in a psychiatric institution in Nice, where at least he was looked after and fed.

Back in Istanbul, as the war ended, Garabed, now over ninety, had died. Ara, Vahan's younger brother, had accordingly returned from Egypt to take over the business. During their childhood, Raffi, Vahan's younger brother, had always 'taken' from Vahan. It was Vahan, three years older than him, who had taught him how to master and ride a horse – how to balance on a bicycle – how to stamp down the snow in the well during the winter in order to make ice for the summer. It was Vahan who shielded him so often from their father's bad temper, which sometimes flared up. It was Vahan who set them all up again in Constantinople when they returned from the deportations. Raffi, in return, had respected his elder brother, even loved him, but had taken it all for granted as younger brothers will, and had even been a little jealous of him.

But Raffi was dead and it was Ara who would have to do something for his shattered and vulnerable brother, barely surviving in an institution in France. So it was Ara, the younger adopted brother, who set off in the middle of 1946 as Europe still lay in waste. The trains were starting to run again, but the situation in Yugoslavia was such that a journey on the old Simplon-Orient was still impossible. It had to be by boat to Marseille.

Ara was an uncomplicated man. The traumatic events of his childhood and the terrible slaughter of his parents and all his siblings in front of his eyes had not affected his adulthood. He loved the man who had saved and then adopted him during those terrible events in 1915, the father of

Vahan and Raffi. He loved his adopted brothers without reserve.

It was a difficult journey for Ara to make. He was not well educated and he knew no other language other than Turkish and Armenian. He was met in Marseille by the indefatigable Jean Grimaud, and was driven in the doctor's battered old citroen to Vahan's old flat in the city of Nice where he was to stay. Then on that same day he was driven to the rather grim Institution set in the hills in the northern suburbs of the city, in which Vahan occupied a spartan little room. He was shown how to get there by himself on public transport. Vahan lived ln that little room, spending his days staring out of the window, eating sparingly, and having twice-weekly sessions with a not very sympathetic psychiatrist.

What Ara then did – repayment for all the kindness shown to him by all the Asadourian family, but coming from his heart – was to sit day by day in Vahan's room until it was time for bed. He would then leave him to return to the flat in the city, but would be back first thing the next morning. For a whole week, nothing at all was said between them, beyond Vahan's acknowledgement of his presence. Vahan was not mad, he had a clear grasp on reality, but he craved punishment for his sins of commission and omission.

In the second week, he did more than just acknowledge Ara, but began nodding, making short comments and showing his pleasure at his arrival each day. Eventually in the third week as Ara sat patiently alongside, Vahan began to talk. Once he began, he could not stop. It all poured out – all the details of his life with Nerissa – his hopes for Hakim – everything. At first Ara only listened, but then as the guilt and the regrets poured out, Ara began replying. What he didn't know about the techniques of psychiatry, he made up for with his love and his absolute honesty, and these virtues came through to the suffering Vahan. Of course, having lived through the two great twentieth century refutations of the theory of the essential goodness of human beings – namely the deportations and massacres of the Armenians in 1915 and the recent equally horrific deportations and killing of the Jews – Vahan was not going to be able to return to his liberal humanist beliefs overnight. On the other hand, the warmth, the essential goodness of this fellow human being, sitting with him day after day, began to penetrate the dark mists in his mind.

Then one day, after yet another week had passed, in the middle of a story about a trip he had made with Hakim and Nerissa round the harbour in the Vieux Port, Vahan suddenly stopped and at last, at last, the tears began to flow. His whole body began to shake with great heaving sobs. Then, and also for the first time in over a month of patient listening, Ara jumped up and sat on the bed next to Vahan and held him tight as Vahan sobbed without stopping for a single moment for over a full hour.

Three days later Vahan, left the Institution. He

would never again be the same confident liberal humanist as he had been, but then neither would most of the rest of society – but he would pick up the threads of his life again. A week later he and Ara said good-bye to the Grimaud family and returned to Istanbul.

Hakim the Jew and Nerissa the Armenian went to their deaths with their arms clasped tightly round each other.

The Israeli government today is one of the few democratic governments in the world which does not recognise the massacres and deportation of the Armenians in 1915 as a crime against humanity.

Epilogue

In October 1940, only a few months after the armistice was signed and a new government operating from Vichy was formed, a series of anti-Semitic laws were passed by that government, starting with the 'Statut des Juifs'. The first of these laws defined a Jew and then went on to ever more discriminatory decrees. The new laws gave authority for the internment of Jews, mainly 'foreign' Jews, but also including native French-born citizens who were Jewish. Several desperately miserable internment camps were set up, not only in the occupied zone, but also in the unoccupied zone. All these laws, first defining who was a Jew, then identifying them in the community by lists prepared by the administration, then interning them preparatory to deportation, were all passed without any overt pressure from the German occupiers.

These camps were guarded and administered by French Gendarmes and police. The fact, the absolutely incontrovertible fact, was that the Germans only had about 2,000 policemen available throughout the whole of France. The French police numbered over 120,000 and without their clear collaboration a good proportion of the internment and deportation of the French and foreign Jews would have been quite impossible.

The worst and largest camp was Drancy just north-west of Paris. After the Vel d'Hiv round-up, Drancy became the main internment camp in the occupied zone. Conditions in that camp and, indeed, in most of the others were catastrophic – the result both of neglect and of active and deliberate ill-will. No beds, no heating, no toilets or clean water – hundreds died. Those that survived were deported in trains consisting of over 40 cattle trucks which trundled their way across Europe to Auschwitz. The first convoy to Auschwitz left on the 27th March 1942. There were 67 such convoys altogether. The last one from Drancy left on 17th August 1944, the last one from the whole of France left from Clermont Ferrand on the 22nd August 1944 after Paris had already been liberated.

These camps were almost all completely staffed and run by French administrators and French police. In the case of Drancy, undoubtedly the worst of the camps, the camp was only finally taken over by the SS at the end of the summer of 1943 when the French staff was dismissed. All in all about 60,000 Jews including a substantial number of children under the age of ten were interned there and deported. Less than three per cent of those deported returned or were ever heard of again. Altogether over 77,000 Jews, 9000 of whom were old men and women, and 8000 small children, were deported from France.

Vichy was not just complying with German demands. As a government it passed laws quite independently of any German pressure, defining who was a Jew. It then isolated them, numbered them, directed clear French government propaganda against them and it then interned them and facilitated their journey to their death. Vichy assistance was crucial in all stages of the liquidation of the Jews living in France.

After the war Vichy officials claimed that they knew nothing of the killings. Laval is supposed to have said to a Protestant leader who remonstrated with him about the deportations, that the Jews were being sent to Eastern Europe to be employed in 'farming colonies'. It was all a complete fallacy. They knew precisely what was the likely end of those train convoys. Vichy France did less to stop the deportations of Jews than almost any other country throughout occupied Europe. The record of Denmark needs no elaboration. Over 90% of the Jewish population there were spirited away across the water to Sweden by the combined effort of their citizens, and with the full cooperation of the Danish leaders. But several other countries too stood up against the various pressures that were exerted. In particular, the record of the Italians is in stark contrast. When the Italians took over the area in the south, east of the River Rhone, as their occupied zone, it immediately became a safe zone for French Jews. The Italian administration saved at least 10,000 French Jews and turned a blind eye to their disappearance over the Swiss border. This went on until the surrender of Italy and the complete take-over of the area by the Germans. In the end not a single Jew was handed over to the Germans by the army or the civil administration of the Kingdom of Italy.

The family that Vahan watched in Paris on that day of the first round-up on 16th July was a refugee family originally from Poland. Their name was Muller and Annette's little brother was called Michael. In due course most of the children rounded up on that day were forcibly separated from their mothers by French police. The screaming and crying totally overwhelmed the gendarmes who tried to drag the children from their mothers. But eventually the levelling of rifles and the setting up of a machine gun settled the issue. Rather than see their children shot, the women pushed them away and were then taken away to Drancy without them.

In the original camp, life without their mothers, or indeed any adults, became sordid in the extreme. The children, virtually abandoned, with nothing to eat but weak soup occasionally doled out, became filthy, suffered from diarrhoea, got into pointless fights with each other over scraps of food, and died. Eventually most of them too ended up in Drancy. This is not dramatic fiction; we know all this because Michael and Annette Muller survived and have told their story. When Vahan heard Annette's mother whisper to her two 10 and 11 year old boys to run away, he was horrified that she had acted against all her instincts to drive away her children so that they might survive.

Every one of the 4,000 small children deported from France between 1942 and 1944 died at Auschwitz, and almost every one of them had been rounded up by the Vichy police. The last convoy left Drancy on the 17th August 1944, only 8 days before the liberation of Paris.

Vahan was deeply pro-French, as indeed are most Armenians. Many Armenians were given refuge by the maligned Third Republic after the terrible deportations of hundreds of thousands of them by the Turks during the Great War. After witnessing the horrors of the Vel d'Hiv round-up, he had cried out in anguish to Nerissa – "What the hell has happened to this tolerant and liberal people."

After the liberation, de Gaulle took the very reasonable line that it would be best for the future of France if a veil was drawn over what had occurred during the Vichy years. A few, notoriously Laval himself, were tried and executed in the first year – but only a very few. Then, until the release of Ophul's documentary –"Le chagrin et la pitié" over 20 years later, no one in France referred to or discussed the Vichy years. In fairness to de Gaulle, even he drew the line at accepting the senior figures of the Catholic church who had presided during the days of Vichy. At the great solemn Mass held at the Notre Dame in Paris a day or two after the liberation, he not only refused to allow Cardinal Suchard – the Cardinal Archbishop of Paris – to preside, he barred him from even entering his own Cathedral, and made sure with the use of armed soldiers that he would be forcibly prevented if he tried.

The charge against Vichy is 'betrayal'.

Betrayal of the principles of liberty, equality and fraternity; betrayal of the social system of Republican France based on civil liberties and equality before the law; betrayal of the British ally by an armistice that broke the treaty obligations between the two countries; betrayal of the minorities living within its borders and under its protection; in the end betrayal of all those deeply committed Francophiles throughout Europe who could say with unconscious irony –

"Nous sommes trahis."

www.ingramcontent.com/pod-product-compliance
Lightning Source LLC
Chambersburg PA
CBHW020235260626
47156CB00002B/691